THE FLOW

Dosia McKay

This is a work of fiction. Names, characters, places, and incidents either are the product of the author's imagination or are used fictitiously, and any resemblance to actual persons, living or dead, businesses, companies, events, or locales is entirely coincidental.

www.DosiaMcKay.com

Editing by Constance Renfrow
Proofreading by Sara Kelly
Cover illustration by Dosia McKay,
based on a photograph by Peter Herrmann

Published by Gavia Music
Knoxville, TN
USA

ISBN 978-1-7341225-1-0 (hardback)
ISBN 978-1-7341225-0-3 (paperback)
Library of Congress Control Number: 2019917753

1

Numbness does not have to be destructive. Its lukewarm embrace can be nourishing, sustaining, prove wonderfully protective. When all other emotions have failed, numbness remains to offer a guiltless escape. It makes no demands. It makes no promises. It accepts everything. It filters in the "What?" without the "How?" or, heaven forbid, the "Why?" Numbness allows just enough depth perception to get around but spares one the drama and the onslaught of glaring colors, sharp contrasts, and decisive statements. There is no need to experience deeply or to express oneself fully, since any deviation from indifference appears completely absurd.

To Claudia, the mysteriousness of the evening fog on the river and the quiet breaking of the water beneath the ferry's bow seemed a waste of nature's creative resources. She was unmoved by them and found comfort in not caring, in not having to notice the intricacies of the velvety green vegetation that covered the riverbanks or the brown-and-gray rooftops of the wooden cottages scattered along.

She wasn't curious about her surroundings and so did not try to soak them in as any newcomer would. It was liberating to feel no obligation to stare all around, or to expend mental energy on the optimal framing of photographs, or to commit to memory any trivial details. She had no strength to amuse herself. The slow passage was for her nothing but one giant sigh, a push away from the world that had rendered her entirely depleted.

The ferry was small enough to wobble with every turn. It wiggled between the islands like a young salmon in summer, eager to taste the ocean for the first time, so that one might think it a sightseeing vessel rather than one built for transport. Its constant, restless rocking and jittering made Claudia nauseous.

Only a few other passengers were on board. A couple leaned on the starboard rail, turning their faces to the setting sun. An elderly man read a newspaper on the bench at the stern. The ferry captain stood in his small steering cabin, the door swinging wide open. Though the word "captain" was undoubtedly too much of a stretch for this unshaven man in overalls whose straps were fastened with one loose button.

"We stop at Overlook Island first, and then I'll drop you off at Watershed, lady!" he shouted to Claudia, leaning out of the cabin.

Claudia nodded, smiling, or maybe grimacing against the blinding sun. For someone so numb inside, she was still acutely susceptible to external stimuli. She had been warned the weather this August would be cool on the St. Lawrence River but had not expected the air to be so piercing. That the boat was traveling straight against the wind intensified the chill. She pulled the sleeves of her brown windbreaker over her knuckles and regretted that she hadn't brought a hat or at least a hairband to keep in check her long and unruly red hair.

The boat slowed as it approached the shore. On the embankment, a row of herring gulls awaited the spectacle. The ferryman lowered the ramp, and the passengers clambered down to the asphalt pier without so much as a glance behind. A few cars drove by. Life carried on in all directions. Then, after a few moments, he raised the ramp, and the ferry gurgled as it pulled backward from the dock, spewing fumes from the exhaust. When they had reached a safe distance from the bank, the vessel was shifted into the forward gear and, with a wide left turn, drew a white circle of a wave onto the water's still, dark green plane.

Claudia was relieved. A typical introvert, she always felt lighter when even small groups of people around her dispersed, and now she had the boat almost entirely to herself. She hoped the captain wouldn't try to initiate conversation, and though he seemed lost in his own thoughts, absentmindedly patting his pockets for his cigarettes and lighter, Claudia moved away from the steering cabin, as if to distance herself from the fumes.

Only a few cottages dotted these riverbanks, and a flock of ducks frolicked between the carcasses of black driftwood that littered a large and muddy beach. They nibbled on the remains of shrubbery and poked their beaks into the mire in search of snails. The water current must have been stronger here, because the boat struggled to keep its course, without being swept to either side, and Claudia held on tightly to the railing. The wind rippled and creased the river's surface, so that it looked like a discarded page from an abandoned sketch of music or an opening of a novel that did not hold any promise.

"That's Watershed!" the captain shouted over the engine noise and pointed farther ahead and to the right. "I have to go around, and we'll dock on the other side."

The island's bank was steep and inaccessible. Tall coniferous trees crept all the way to the edge, exposing their hanging roots in a cross section of the red soil eroded by the river. A few birds flew into the branches, but Claudia didn't know to what species they belonged or what might be their habits. It made no difference to her. The boat edged neatly into a channel that led to the center of the bay, where a small wooden pier was perched, with a gravel road that stretched away into the forest. The island looked more secluded than she had anticipated. A lone blue Chevy truck, which hadn't seen its glory days since the 1980s, was parked farther up the road. Its driver climbed out, slammed the door behind him, and walked toward the docking ferry. Claudia gathered her small suitcase, her laptop bag, and her large black portfolio, preparing to disembark; then she stepped onto the pier.

"Hi, I'm Victor. The house isn't that far, but since it's getting dark, I thought I would give you a ride up the hill."

"Claudia. Thank you." She pulled her suitcase over the gravel, following him.

"How was your trip?" he asked, turning back but not slowing down.

"Uneventful. And long." She wasn't keen on stretching the conversation beyond the bare minimum required.

"Oh yes. Where are you coming from?"

"Hoboken."

"So, the train and then the bus?" He kept his hands in his pockets.

"Yes, exactly," she said, without looking up, trying to watch her step.

When they reached the truck, Victor didn't offer to help lift her luggage into the bed, but Claudia didn't struggle. She had only packed the essentials and a few random items, since the last few days had been rather improvised. The artist retreat coordinator had notified Claudia of the sudden opening—caused by a cancellation—but Claudia delayed committing to the spot until the last possible minute. When it came to packing, she hadn't given much thought to appropriate attire or the weather forecast.

"Is that a drawing portfolio?" Victor pointed to the large black folio.

"Yes, it is. But I don't keep any drawings inside."

"What then? Treasure maps?"

Claudia smiled politely.

"Just some large manuscript paper."

"You're a writer, then?" he asked, as he climbed into the driver's seat.

"I'm a composer. I like to sketch my musical ideas on large sheets of staff paper," Claudia replied, situating herself in the passenger seat and fastening her seatbelt.

"But I see you also have your laptop with you. Not averse to technology, then?"

"I like computers, but there are times when nothing beats a simple pencil. Whatever aids the creative process."

"I hear you."

He turned to look through the cab's rear window and backed the truck out of the spot. He was a tall man in his thirties, skinny but muscular. His thin hands were riddled with bulging blue veins in the same way the uneven road was crisscrossed with narrow tree roots. Dressed in a loose black T-shirt and black cotton pants covered in dust, he gave the impression of someone who might work outdoors, but his soft face and dark wavy hair that fell to his cheekbones betrayed a more sheltered life. He drove slowly over the gravel, lazily leaning his forearms on the steering wheel as he squinted at the road ahead.

It might help to turn on the headlights, Claudia thought—after all, it was nearly dusk—but she wasn't about to instruct him. She was too tired to care. She hoped to see the house emerge at any minute now, so that she could finally stop being shaken, jolted, tossed, and swayed.

If there were any buildings along the way, Claudia couldn't see them through the dense forest. Thorny blackberry bushes stretched from the road into the thicket, and the pines towered in the background. The road branched a couple of times, and an unexpected clearing revealed a large patch of soft grass that looked well cared for, though uncut. The island, clearly, was much larger than she had supposed.

"Here we are," said Victor.

Watershed Villa appeared on the left. Its brown and weathered cedar-shake siding contrasted with the gray stone foundation and metal roof. Wide concrete stairs flanked by two stone columns led to a spacious veranda that stretched the length of the façade. The house had one level and possibly an attic, judging by the steep pitch of the roof. It wasn't opulent or extravagant, yet everything about it spoke of solid craftsmanship and elegance. Warm, soft light emanated through the windows, and a vast courtyard stretched from the bottom of the stairs all the way to the forest's edge. It was paved with tightly compacted gravel that, over the years, had sunk deep into the soil, forming a smooth abstract mosaic. There was no landscaping to speak of, no flowerbeds or obligatory suburban shrubs. Instead, the forest crept in from the back with its lush, flowering grasses, green herbs, thorny branches, and unwieldy climbers, creating around the building a quiet nest.

"I'll drop you off here," the driver said, pointing to the entrance, "and will catch up with you later. I have to park the truck in the shed. Feel free to head straight in."

Claudia pulled her luggage out of the truck bed and up the veranda stairs. She opened the heavy wooden door, revealing a spacious hallway.

2

The first thing she noticed upon entering was the smell. It was the fragrance of aged wood and paper. Not the musty odor of an old person's parlor or of fur coats, but an aura of legacy, tradition one might encounter in historic libraries, violin workshops, or leather furniture stores. But here was also a hint of coffee beans and floor wax, intermingled with nutmeg, juniper, and sage.

Claudia dropped her belongings by the ornamental wood paneling and proceeded to look around. She walked past a round hall table, whose glossy surface displayed only a miniature silver box and reflected light of a stained-glass lamp. Off to the right was an office with a stately honey colored desk, a matching wooden swivel chair, and a row of bookcases that lined the entire far wall. Down the hall, Claudia found an open room, a sunroom perhaps, but it was too late and too dark to appreciate the floor-to-ceiling windows. A small worktable and a couple of easels were gathered in the center, while an oversize leather sofa with velvet pillows was pushed to the side. A worn oriental rug and an armchair marked a sitting space in front.

Wall sconces softly illuminated the room as the furniture cast shadows on the dark orange-and-brown walls. The dining room to the left featured an oblong formal table that could seat at least eight. A tall buffet and two curio cabinets, housing a display of patterned porcelain, completed the layout.

Finally, there was a spacious library, and Claudia gasped at the wealth of the collection. Thick art volumes filled with reproductions of Rothko, Pollock, Rivera, O'Keefe, and Picasso. Dictionaries, atlases, compendiums, fiction, poetry, philosophy. A cursory scan registered such names as Seneca, Flaubert, Du Bois, Hugo, Mann, Pushkin, Dickinson, and Plotinus, all organized neatly in custom-built shelving made of polished wood. Countless vinyl records, as many compact discs, and an entire alphabetized section of music scores were divided into the chamber and orchestral compositions. By the window, leather armchairs were gathered around a massive black Bösendorfer grand piano.

Claudia would gladly have sunk into one of the plush chairs and traveled to another world with the aid of one of the atlases. But even without opening any of them, she already felt she had entered a new reality. Accustomed to fluorescent lighting, industrial carpet, and particle-board furniture, here Claudia sensed a shift in her mood. She had an inkling that she had made the right decision in coming here. Maybe this place would offer her the change of scenery she so desperately needed.

"Oh, I see you found your way in," a soft, feminine voice spoke behind her.

Claudia turned and faced a frail elderly woman. Her light—but not quite gray—hair was clasped in a bun and framed her well-preserved features. Beneath a white kitchen apron, she wore a beige turtleneck and a pair of silky black trousers. Elegant house shoes and a pearl bracelet completed her stylish outfit.

"I'm Bertha. Welcome to Watershed."

"It's nice to meet you, Bertha. I'm Claudia."

"I prefer Ms. Bertha, dear."

Claudia instantly regretted her familiarity, but the woman didn't seem to dwell on the gaffe. She motioned for Claudia to follow her into the kitchen.

"You must be very tired and hungry. I left some food for you in the fridge." The woman moved confidently but shakily in front of Claudia. "After you settle in, feel free to reheat it." She took from a cabinet a dinner plate and a glass, which she set on the small kitchen table. "I understand you will be staying for six weeks?"

"Yes, ma'am," Claudia answered dutifully.

"Good. Let me quickly give you a few rules of the house." She removed a blue fabric napkin from a drawer and added it to the place setting. "I serve breakfast at eight o'clock. Tomorrow, you can tell me more about your food preferences. You are on your own when it comes to lunch, but, of course, feel free to use whatever you find in the refrigerator or the pantry. I only ask that you clean up after yourself and don't leave dirty dishes in the sink."

Though her face had a soft glow, her eyes were penetrating, and she looked Claudia over from top to bottom.

"I serve dinner at five o'clock, but if you don't show up, I will save you some for later. I don't expect you to eat with me every day, dear." She waved her arm and smiled. "God knows you artists follow your own schedule. I stay for the most part in the west wing of the house and won't interfere with your activities. So, make yourself at home and don't feel like you have to entertain me. I have plenty to keep me occupied." She took off her apron and hung it up inside the pantry. "But if you need me for any reason, you can easily find me."

She led Claudia back into the main hallway.

"Your bedroom is upstairs, and you will find fresh towels in the bathroom. I like to wash the sheets every Saturday. The laundry room is near the pantry. Feel free to use it as you need to. You may come and go as you please." She straightened a decorative quilt depicting an emerald stream and tall grasses, which had been draped over the back of a bench near the stairwell. "Of course, you know there is no Internet here."

Had Claudia known this? Had she overlooked this detail?

"But the cell phone reception is decent. I doubt

you will be bored here. There is always something to do on the island. I know you will want to venture into the forest." She adjusted a small abstract painting on the side table. "And don't worry about locking the front door. We are perfectly safe here." She turned back to Claudia. "Well, I suppose that's all for now. I will let you freshen up and get some rest. Goodnight, dear." And with that, she smiled, turned, and walked abruptly away.

Claudia was grateful Ms. Bertha hadn't asked her to recite her life story and was glad to be finally left alone. She wasn't sure she needed a full meal but would welcome a cup of tea or warm soup. But first, she wanted to inspect her room. She climbed the wooden staircase, sliding her hand on the cold iron railing, intricately wrought in the shape of branching vines. Upstairs she found a spacious bedroom with a four-poster bed, a simple ash table that functioned as a desk, a couple of chairs, and a deep armchair. She sat on the edge of the bed and was pleasantly surprised by the soft and comfortable mattress. She lifted the corner of the bedding to find pillow-top padding underneath. She couldn't believe her luck.

3

After unpacking her toiletries and splashing warm water on her face, Claudia went downstairs in search of a late dinner. She poked around the kitchen and opened a few drawers to familiarize herself with the setup. In the refrigerator, Ms. Bertha had left a Tupperware box and a bowl labeled with Claudia's name. One contained roast beef and broccoli, the other tomato soup. She poured the soup into a ceramic dish, intending to reheat it quickly, but discovered there was no microwave anywhere. The outdated cabinets stored only pots, spices, an archaic food processor, and a few cookbooks. She would have to use the stovetop, so she poured the soup into a small saucepan and stirred it impatiently as it was slowly warming up.

When she sat down at the small square table, she heard an indistinct conversation from the other end of the house. Muffled laughter, a woman's voice, another voice—a man's. Evening guests, perhaps? Ms. Bertha's neighbors?

Victor entered the kitchen and smiled at Claudia, who was twiddling her spoon between her middle and index fingers.

"Ah, there you are! Come on, let me introduce you to the others."

Claudia didn't feel like moving, but since he was already on his way out and she didn't want to be rude on the first day, she stood up.

"Come on, bring your food with you," he said. "We are in the dining room."

She picked up her soup bowl and reluctantly followed him through to the dining room, where, at the end of the large oak table, sat a young woman and an older chubby man.

"Welcome, *Primavera!*" the man exclaimed energetically, rising to greet her.

"This is Claudia, a composer," Victor introduced her.

"Nice to meet you," Claudia said, waving awkwardly and then setting her bowl on the table.

"I'm Stephanie." The girl offered a handshake.

"And I'm Diego," the chubby man added, straightening his loose-fitting gray shirt.

"Diego is a painter," said Victor. "Soon he'll beg you to pose for him, and then he'll force you to hold a contorted position for hours. He is a sadist."

Diego laughed loudly. His hair was shaved close to his scalp, leaving only a thin layer of blondish fuzz. He didn't look like the painterly type, Claudia decided. She turned to the young woman, whose tight blue dress revealed a physique that was grotesquely voluptuous, emphasized by a narrow belt that squeezed her perfect hourglass figure.

"And Stephanie is taking a break from her opera auditions. She just got her master's this past spring," Victor said.

"Oh, yeah? Where did you go to school?" Claudia asked, reflexively, and regretting the question as soon as she spoke it. She hated comparing pedigrees.

"I got a full ride at Brandon-Wells. I have been auditioning all summer in Austria and Italy," Stephanie said proudly, brushing her large brown ringlets from her plump, olive-complexioned cheeks.

"Oh, wow!" Claudia gushed, with an overenthusiastic grin, but inwardly she was rolling her eyes.

"And I'm a writer," Victor said.

Wait a minute. Wasn't she supposed to be the only artist here? Claudia couldn't quite remember. She had applied to several residencies on a whim and had failed to keep track of what each program offered. She should have double-checked before accepting. Still, at least she had her own private room and workspace. She hoped the others wouldn't disturb her too much. If she played it well, she could make this less-than-ideal situation work. For now, the best course of action was to remain as amicable as possible.

"I'm sorry. I should have asked you earlier in the truck. Are you a grad student?" Claudia took her seat, and the others followed suit, arranging themselves in a half circle.

"Oh, no, I've been out of school for a while. I received the Preston Fellowship last year. Now I'm between a couple of projects."

"Don't be so modest," said Diego. "Victor just won the Kesselman Prize in Literary Fiction. His books are getting hot. Isn't your publisher planning a book tour for next year?"

"Maybe. I don't know yet. I have to finish the novel first," Victor answered quickly, dismissing Diego.

"And what about you, Claudia?" Stephanie asked.

"Well, I'm a doctoral student at Grayland State University, and I lecture there as well. I was able to squeeze in this retreat before the fall semester starts." Feeling a bit warm, Claudia rolled up the sleeves of her green blouse, revealing her pale, thin forearms.

"What's your doctoral thesis on?" Stephanie pressed.

"Melodic Development in the Works of Serialist Composers in the Mid-Twentieth Century," Claudia recited.

"Sounds interesting. I would like to hear more about that sometime," said Stephanie politely.

"What about you, Diego?" Claudia deflected attention away from herself.

"Oh, Diego is a moocher off wealthy patrons. They eat up his landscapes like cupcakes."

Stephanie rested her arm on the back of his chair, giggling girlishly.

"Well, I can't complain at the moment. Between them and a few grants and residencies, I stay afloat." He rested his hands on his bulging stomach. "But I tell you, there is nothing like Watershed to get your creative juices flowing. I come here for what I call 'character landscapes.' Man, have you seen the sunset on the river today?" Squinting, he glided his right hand horizontally across the air. "Late August—it's the best. There's just something about the light that shifts the colors this time of the year. I brought plenty of umber paint, for sure." He oozed excitement. "Sorry to blab on about my work. Tell her what you're doing, baby."

"Well," Stephanie began slowly, "this is my first time here, and I don't have a definite project in mind, but I do want to branch out into other musical forms beyond the opera. I have been listening more to purely instrumental music, and I just feel like I should be entering a new chapter. To reinvent myself, somehow."

"Do you mean to explore chamber music or art songs?" Claudia asked.

"Maybe. I don't know. It's hard to explain."

"And what about you, Victor? What are you working on here?"

"I'm writing a speculative fiction novel that might become a psychological thriller. I haven't made up my mind yet." He leaned back in his chair, resting his ankle over his knee and folding his arms behind his head.

"What's the difference between the two?" Claudia asked.

"In the psychological thriller, the characters would be more deranged." He looked at Diego, then burst out laughing. The others joined him.

"Go for it, man! You never hold back, do you?" Diego said, amused. "Warp those bastards' reality!" They high-fived each other triumphantly. "I love his books."

Victor turned back to Claudia. "And do you have a specific project you will be working on?"

"A cello sonata. I have written music for the violin, viola, and the string orchestra before, but never for cello solo," she said confidently, having rehearsed the fictitious pitch earlier. She swung her foot under the table. "It feels like the timing and the setting are perfect for it." She recited her lines so smoothly while nodding her head in agreement, she almost convinced herself.

4

The next morning, Claudia woke up unusually rested. The plush, warm bedding must have done the trick, or was it the immensely deep silence of her surroundings? For the first time, she had been able to hear the gentle swooshes of tiny blood vessels in her skull. She also noticed other noises she had never discerned in the big city: the creaking of wooden walls, the beating of moth wings against the lampshade, the tapping of a lizard's feet on the windowpane. Although she hadn't set her alarm, the sun delicately woke her when its pinkish glow filtered through the green branches of the forest.

And the forest! Now, in the daylight, she saw the vastness of it. Two large windows, devoid of any draperies or blinds, one near the desk, and the other one diagonally across, on the other side of the bed, allowed Claudia an unrestricted view of the outdoors. The trees were practically inside her room, pushing in, knocking on the panes, reaching for her with their tendrils.

She stood and stretched, looking down onto the courtyard below. There was a wooden bench at the end of the stone veranda, a scraggly patch of vegetable garden, an old moss-covered shed, and a pile of firewood stacked neatly under a detached awning. A few brown leaves rustled on the porch roof. Specks of yellow and reddish foliage punctuated the greenery of the canopies, hinting at the season's imminent change. She should get outside and find the clearing she saw yesterday. It couldn't be far away. And how big was this island, anyway? Claudia slowly pulled on a pair of green sweatpants, a T-shirt, and a light brown sweater, and without giving any thought to grooming or breakfast, walked down the stairs and out into the cold air.

She walked along the gravel road from yesterday. If she happened upon any of the branching side roads, she decided she might take one, but she didn't intend to be gone for long. For now, she merely wanted to lose herself within the woodland, to be truly alone from the rest of the world.

Her nostrils detected the rich and calming smell of water. This wasn't moldy or muddy like a marsh, nor was it salty and sour like the ocean. It was distinctly clear and pure, like gray clouds, silver rain, wet moss; the fragrance of clarity, honesty. She let it pull her in.

It seemed she could reach the dock from here, but if she went all the way down the hill, she would then have to climb it right back up in order to return to the villa. She hesitated. Instead, she walked off the path into the thicket, looking up into the sky and attempting to see to the very tips of the trees. Their trunks, straight and narrow, encircled her in a radial array, pointing to the precise center above her head. She stared into that opening, imagining what it would be like to be sucked up into that hole and transported to another realm. She wouldn't mind disappearing right there, right then. Of all the ways she had yet envisioned her death, this was the most farfetched. She added it to her mental catalog of painless and efficient demises.

Or what about simply lying down underneath some ferns or hollies? Was that not what animals did when they sensed their time had come? She could fall asleep and rest. And rest some more, and sink deeper and wider and stronger, until she didn't feel anymore. The plants would swallow her, the roots would receive her nourishment, and the herbaceous layer would slowly assimilate her carcass. The forest would distill from her all the chemical compounds, all the minerals it needed for its growth, leaving behind pristinely clear, pure, transparent, silent, mute water, and a puff of vapor. She could not think of a more poetic way to die.

She was weak and dizzy. Hundreds of dark floating specks punctuated her field of vision, and that was how she was usually reminded she needed to eat something. Occasionally she felt pain or heard growling in her stomach but never true hunger. In its place were only degrees of nausea.

It was time to return to the villa. At 9:15 a.m., it was probably too late to join Ms. Bertha for breakfast but a cup of coffee was all Claudia needed. She started to head back, breathing deeply, hoping she wouldn't faint on the way. She walked up the steps to the veranda and through the front doorway. This time, in the hallway, she noticed old photographs on the walls. In one, a few smiling people gathered at a piano; in another, a woman knelt beside a large dog, petting it; a man held a violin. Portraits of family or friends.

"Ah, there you are! You must be Claudia. Welcome to Watershed." An older man waved to her from the office. "Please, come in for a second. Would you mind?"

He wore a white long-sleeved shirt, an elegant navy blue vest, and a pair of formal trousers. His hair was carefully combed and slicked back. Thin metal spectacles sat low on his nose. He looked over them at Claudia while pressing down his chin but raising his eyebrows. He stretched his arms in a welcoming gesture.

"I'm Richard Holbert, director of the Artist Enrichment Program and liaison for the Watershed Foundation."

"It's nice to meet you, Mr. Holbert," Claudia recited automatically.

"Oh, please, it's Richard." He brimmed with happiness as he motioned for her to walk in front of the desk, while he took tiny steps, his arms still outstretched like those of a penguin.

"We are very pleased to have you here, Claudia. You were chosen from among many applicants, and you come highly recommended. You were certainly our top choice."

Claudia rapidly flapped her eyelashes. That was not how she remembered it.

"Let's take care of just a few formalities, shall we?" He lifted a black briefcase onto the desk and unclasped its shiny silver locks.

"I see you are visiting us from Grayland State University. Very well. A more regional institution, but that can be very beneficial sometimes. Very beneficial." He motioned for her to sit, while he settled himself behind his desk and began to shuffle through paper folders and stacks of punched and bound sheets.

"There you are!" he exclaimed happily, raising his hand to mark the occasion. "Claudia Morton. Age . . . we won't discuss that. We know how you ladies don't like to dwell on those numbers." He was trying to be swift and amusing. A few more shuffles back and forth, and then back again.

"And I see that the university covers your health insurance. That's excellent, excellent. Not that we anticipate any events here on the island, but we, the administrators, like to have our I's crossed and our T's dotted." He appreciated his own sense of humor.

"I see that you are not on a full sabbatical but

simply taking the summer off; is that correct?" He was looking at her over his glasses again. Claudia nodded, pulling at the sleeves of her sweater.

"I know Grayland State likes to have their doctoral assistants work through the summer session, but it's nice they made an exception for you. As they should." He leaned forward and grinned.

"And here is your resume." He slid his index finger from top to bottom. "Five semesters teaching, American Society of Creative . . . musicology conferences, thesis, melodic development, serialist composers, et cetera, et cetera. It's all very much there, I suppose, very much." He opened his arms triumphantly. No one could deny the information was where it was supposed to be.

Claudia uncrossed her legs and re-crossed them the opposite way, while smoothing her sweatpants with her hand. She couldn't for the life of her remember if she had combed her hair.

"So, tell me about this cello sonata you'll be working on." He leaned back in his chair and crossed his arms, looking very comfortable.

"Well," she began, slowly. "I have written music for the violin, the viola, and the string orchestra before, but never for cello solo. It just feels like the timing and the setting are right for it." She made intricate gestures with her hands to give her lines more impact. "In my doctoral thesis, I explore the melodic development of the serialist composers, and I think my music will probe this process." She was glad she had enough mental capacity to recite the formula without any glitches.

"Aha, aha." He continued to look at her with his mouth partly open, gnawing on a pen as one might a cigar.

"But a cello sonata, that's chamber music we're talking about. Usually, when composition fellows come to us,"—he lowered his voice, emphasizing each word—"they tackle larger projects. I don't know—a ballet, an oratorio, a symphony. I certainly don't want to discourage you if a sonata is what you want to work on, but perhaps you would like to reconsider?" Richard leaned toward her. His smile was insistent.

"I'm not sure. My advisor at Grayland approved this project. I don't think I can start from scratch right now, especially since I already have drafts of the sonata." She had nothing and she lied without flinching. It was becoming more natural each time. She couldn't tell Richard she didn't want to work on any project at all, that she was here only to escape, to stall.

"But chamber music, Claudia, chamber music . . ." He pointed to the ceiling with his outstretched fingers as if preparing to sermonize. "The world is changing. Who plays chamber music anymore?" He pursed his lips. "It has been relegated to university recitals. I don't mean to be critical, but in order to be taken seriously as a composer, you should take larger forms into consideration."

She wanted to blurt out that at least with chamber music, she had a chance of having her compositions performed and heard—at the university, maybe even a few other small venues—while it was nearly impossible to secure an orchestral or operatic performance. But, like any experienced academic diplomat, she smiled politely and held her tongue.

"You certainly have a point, Richard. There is no doubt about it. I don't think I'm ready for a symphonic work right now, but I know this is something I will be strongly leaning toward in the future." She was fluent in the institutional lingo. "I have developed an interest in string instruments recently, and I feel the cello sonata is the way to go. At this time." She gave him a piercing stare, as if to say, *I am serious, and this is what I am going to do whether you like it or not.*

"Of course, of course. We are here only to offer guidance and assistance. Please think of me as your temporary adviser, not a replacement for your advisor at Grayland at all." He leaned back into the armchair again. "And I know Greg quite well. He and I go back a long way. A hardworking, patient man—that's what he is."

Richard stood to signal the audience was over, and once again he smiled and stretched his arms, this time to guide her out.

"If there is anything we can do for you, Claudia,

anything at all, please don't hesitate."

5

Anxiety is not a prison. The one who suffers from anxiety is the prison. She is the cage in which the monster is locked. Usually, the beast can be appeased, but sometimes it rages on, demanding to be let out. Anxiety desperately wants to escape, but instinctively, the cage suppresses it instead of setting it free. Anxiety springs in the upper abdomen, spreading its tentacles into the lungs, upper arms, and the bowels. It chokes the neck, softens the knees; it soaks the root of the tongue in bitterness. It nauseates, overpowers, subjugates, neuters. Then, after it has completed its outburst, it dissipates softly through the droplets of sweat on a blood-drained forehead, and tingles the tips of the fingers, as if in a parting gesture. But it never truly leaves. The parasite only retreats to feed off its host until it gathers enough momentum to lash out once again in most mundane settings. At a crowded, harshly-lit grocery store, during teaching of a rudimentary lecture to incoming freshmen, at a restaurant where the only remaining open table is conspicuously located, on a subway temporarily detained between stations.

Claudia's therapist urged her to keep a diary of distressing events. He introduced a point and reward system. Suddenly, every completed phone call became a small victory, and so did any concerts attended till the final bow or conversations initiated with strangers. Every circumstance was an uphill battle, for which strategies were painstakingly drawn and either executed or aborted at the very last minute. Life seemed like something to be conquered, not something to enjoy.

Claudia had tried several anti-anxiety medications. They all helped temporarily but eventually left her in a zombie state, numb and indifferent. They allowed her to function at her university job, but killed all her desire to compose or to pursue any other creative activity. Now, eight months clean of all pharmaceuticals, she still felt mostly tired and dazed.

Because alcohol exacerbated her anxiety, she had radically limited her consumption to the point of avoiding all social engagements outside of work. A rumor spread that she was a recovering alcoholic and not a team player. The more withdrawn she became, the more ostracized she felt. And the lonelier she was, the less she wanted to reach out to others.

She had chosen a path in academia because she longed to be a part of a community of like-minded people. With her extensive knowledge of music theory and art history, her interest in culture and philosophy, a university seemed like a logical choice—a temple of learning in the religion of humanism, a shelter for intellectuals in the middle of the sea of ignorant masses.

But in reality, she had not become a high priestess of art. Instead, she babysat adolescents by ushering them through the labyrinth of course catalogs and class syllabi. Her life became a series of bureaucratic rituals, performed to appease the requirements of the administration. Monthly reports, quarterly projections, retention rates, graduation rates, grade point averages, bell curves, midterms, committees, and memos had taken her further and further from what she really wanted to do: compose.

She didn't find her colleagues could sympathize. Most of her professional relationships were rooted in strategic alliances, potential benefits, likelihoods of tenure, rankings dependent on the number of publications, and exchanges of speaking engagements and paid masterclasses. The currency she dealt in wasn't music; certainly not her own music, and not even her own opinion about the music of others. She often wondered if the system would collapse if the music were removed from it completely, or if it would go blithely on, unaware of its absence.

Now that she was on the verge of applying for full-time positions, she was questioning not only her direction but, indeed, all the scholastic and career choices she had ever made. Was this a natural phase for every doctoral candidate? Would things improve once she completed her thesis? Would her outlook be better at a different school, in another state? Or should she abandon everything and start over before it was too late?

Claudia sat at her desk, pressing her palms against the cold pages of the manuscript paper. She rubbed them flatly as if to warm them. She was horrified by the emptiness of the pages. Although the paper was ruled with neat rows of five-line staves, to her ears, it signified the muteness of a void. If the vertical bar lines had been drawn in at equal spacing, they would at least give the impression of the passing of time or a ticking clock, but without them, it was pure deafness. With her pencil, she doodled something in the corner of the page, a grotesque treble clef branching into incoherent spirals. She switched to the fountain pen, and for a few moments enjoyed the gliding sensation, the flow of dark blue ink, and the scratching of the nib against the paper. But the result was only a childish doodle, the blotches of an imbecile.

Health insurance, student loans, rent, food, tenure, thesis—a litany of tension points cascaded and bounced inside her mind like lotto balls. Claudia sensed the familiar warmth spreading into her lungs. She was dizzy, lightheaded. She knew what to do. She allowed the panic to disperse evenly over her, and then she stepped away from her desk and stumbled into the bathroom. She shoved away the bath rug, pulled off her sweatshirt, and lay down in the fetal position on the floor's cold tiles. Shivers overtook her in small and large waves. Her legs spasmed, she straightened them, and then she pulled them against her chest. The cool floor anchored her to reality. Her long red hair swept the mosaic tiles, and her tears dripped sideways down her cheek. She knew it would pass. It always had before. She has found a temporary shelter and she would figure it all out. She only needed time.

"Claudia, dear?" Ms. Bertha knocked quietly on Claudia's door. "I truly hate to disturb you, but I don't think you have left your room all day. Are you all right?"

"I'm all right, Ms. Bertha!" Claudia shouted from the bathroom, suppressing her sobbing and wiping her mouth.

"I brought you some tea and a cookie. I will leave them right here." The porcelain dishes and silverware clanked against the wooden floor. Then, the sound of Ms. Bertha's steps receded into silence.

6

Claudia's second night at Watershed wasn't as restful. Nevertheless, she woke early and decided to do something constructive. Even if she couldn't force herself to write music or conduct research, she could focus on her well-being. After all, she didn't know when she would ever spend time in nature again and wished to take full advantage of her island stay. Today, she would try to walk all the way to the dock and maybe from there follow the shore.

As she was leaving the villa, she noticed the door of the shed was ajar. Her first thought was that Victor might be in there, taking the truck for a spin. She peeked in. Inside, a man who seemed to be about her age was frantically searching the drawers of a tall red metal tool chest.

"Hi," he said plainly and gave her only a quick glance.

"Hi. I was just . . ." Caught off guard, she pointed in the direction she was intending to wander.

"I'm Gabriel." He kept pulling open drawers, top to bottom, bending over to look inside, reaching his arm all the way to the back of each one.

"I'm Claudia. Do you work here?"

Clearly, he did. He wore gray cargo pants, a white T-shirt smeared with grease, steel-toe work boots, and a green cotton jacket.

"I'm working on the boat at the dock, and I need a chisel. I should have brought my bag. I guess I'll have to make two trips." His voice had a dark, soothing timbre, and he spoke without looking at her. A couple of plastic tubs, spackle tools, a hammer, a sandwich in a Ziploc bag, and a blue thermos were all scattered on a wooden worktable nearby.

"Do you need a hand? I'm going to the dock if you want help carrying all this." Claudia surprised herself with the offer.

"Yeah?" He turned to face her, and the wrinkling of his forehead gave way to a sudden brightness. "That would be great. Let me get organized here. I think I've almost got it."

He handed her a couple of tools and the thermos but struggled to gather the rest in his arms, so she took a few more things to help him. They headed off down the main road.

"You must be new here. How do you like island life so far?" he asked in a casual tone.

"It certainly has an appeal. I like how quiet and peaceful it is." Claudia could be good at small talk when necessary. "What do you do around here? Do you work for the Foundation?" she asked.

"I mostly help Ms. Bertha. I run errands, bring

her groceries, and take her to the mainland when she needs it. Sometimes I work on her truck."

"And her boat."

"No, it's my boat. She lets me borrow her tools. Here, it's this way." He pointed to a path that branched off to the left.

Claudia stopped in her tracks and looked around, disoriented. "I thought we were going to the dock."

"Yes, but not to the ferry dock. I'm anchored at the small pier."

Claudia hesitated.

"It's just down here on the other side of the hill," he assured her.

"I guess that'll be fine." She wasn't convinced but felt obligated to help him carry his belongings.

"Well," Gabriel asked, convivially, "what about you? What are you doing here?"

"I'm running away." The words startled her, but she kept looking square ahead as if she had meant to say them.

"This is a great place to get lost. There are many other islands around, meandering channels, and canals that never see a living soul. Once, we had a fugitive hiding for ten months in an abandoned house on an island. No one knew he was there until the FBI showed up with helicopter searchlights in the middle of the night. Are you a fugitive?" He grinned at her.

Claudia laughed, but only to keep the

conversation lighthearted. “If I were, would you give me up to the authorities?”

“No, I would smuggle you food,” he answered earnestly.

The dock was barely visible from the path, nearly hidden behind the tall grass. A small motorboat was tied to the pier. Gabriel climbed inside and, after dropping his tools, started to rearrange the plastic coverings, ropes, a life jacket, and the oars.

“Come on, then.” Gabriel reached out his hand to her.

“I thought you were going to work on it. Isn’t there something wrong with the engine?” Claudia lingered on the pier, still holding his thermos and tools.

“The engine is fine. The boat just needs some cosmetic patching.” He withdrew his hand and instead cleared a space on the bench, pushing aside a rain jacket, a sweater, and a book.

Knowing better than to entrust her safety to a stranger in a secluded place, Claudia hesitated.

“Come on, I’ll help you escape.” He bent down to shuffle through a toolbox, his back turned.

What was the worst that could possibly happen? He could kill her and drop her body in the river. He might even do her a favor. Claudia stepped in. He offered her a life vest, but she declined it.

“Where do you want to go? What would you like to see?” he asked calmly.

"I don't care. Anywhere is fine." She didn't look at him and seated herself on the bench.

The boat was small, but its engine was powerful and swift. Gabriel maneuvered it effortlessly. They followed the inlet slowly and carefully until they reached a wider opening, and when finally they hit the open water, Claudia gasped at the abrupt gust of wind. The speed intensified the chill, causing her to shiver.

"Is this too fast for you? It can be very cold against the wind." He offered her a jacket.

"No, it's fine. The cold air helps me. I mean, it feels good," she replied, without turning back, holding tight to the rail.

She was facing the bow as he navigated from the stern. They went for a long time in silence. The river spilled wider, splitting into two distinct corridors. A large island plowed through the belly of the river's flow, with barely any signs of erosion on its stone bank. The ground was different up here: greenish stones mixed with sparkling brown sand. The waves became rougher, and the boat jumped a few times over the water's surface. Gabriel seemed to sense Claudia's discomfort, because he slowed, turning toward a connecting creek. The air temperature rose as soon as they reached the coast's shelter from the wind.

"I'll show you a hidden treasure," he offered.

They passed along the shoreline, beneath kneeling trunks and low-hanging maple branches.

Here the water was still and clear all the way to the bottom, revealing a labyrinthine tangle of root wad. He killed the engine, allowing the boat to drift with the current, and standing on the transom, he began to paddle with a long oar. When they reached the trunk of a white birch growing horizontally over the water, he pushed with the oar away from it, into the center of the riverbed. The boat drifted silently across the channel. The sun wove a shiny web on the myriad of wavelets. He submerged the oar to slow their movement and to adjust their course.

"It's down here," said Gabriel, pointing to the depths beneath them.

Below, the skeleton of a shipwreck was lying on its side. They floated quietly above it. Its rusted windows and railing retained splotches of orange-and-blue paint. The dance of water currents caused the shapes to twist and morph as if in a magic magnifying glass. The boat seemed too large to fit properly in this channel.

"It's been down there for nearly seventy years. The riverbed was different then, but even in those days, this stretch was too dangerous for larger vessels," Gabriel said.

"I wonder what made the boat lose its course."

"Bad weather, lack of respect for the river and its ways, outdated maps. No one remembers anymore."

They reached deeper waters where the neighboring tributaries spilled in unison into a rough, bubbly confluence. Gabriel restarted the engine and turned the boat around. This time, they rode with the wind and the smells and the sensations of movement changed. They passed an island whose bank was crumbling and unstable. Some deciduous trees leaned on its edge, their partially exposed roots struggling to anchor them to the soil. Others were already lying flat on the beach below. The strata of sediment varied in color from muddy gray through black, dark brown, light umber, and beige. The boat slowed again as it came closer to the shore, drifting along.

The sun warmed their backs, and Claudia finally turned to face Gabriel. He was looking to the side, lost in his own thoughts. He stood on the transom again, oar in hand, inspecting the shoreline. He was tall, with muscular arms and large strong hands. Neither handsome nor distasteful, he was merely ordinary. And yet, Claudia thought, there was something intriguing about him. His ease and patience. The way he pushed the water in a calculated and laborious manner that seemed effortless. He gave an impression of a hunter or a scout, as if he could lie still in wait for his prey for hours on end. He didn't seem to feel the need to talk incessantly, to amuse her, to impress her. He was simply there, carried by the water yet navigating it at will, bending it to his whims. He was in control without having to be in control.

He guided the boat toward another canal. This

one narrower, marshy, hedged on both sides by tall cattail sedge and soft rush. They drifted again in silence as Gabriel, from time to time, gave the boat a strong push. The water was very shallow here, and Claudia worried they might get stuck.

"Look to your right," Gabriel whispered. He was crouched down.

A single gray heron stood at the edge of the river, tall and elegant. It watched them and monitored their movement but didn't flinch or fly away. It didn't seem to be fishing.

"What's he doing?" Claudia asked, quietly leaning forward.

"He's waiting for us to leave him alone. Herons are one of only a few bird species that spend extensive time away from their partners after their offspring leave the nest. They hunt in solitude and don't chase their prey. They let it come to them."

The bird unexpectedly spread its wings, and with a whoosh, it took off right above their heads. It looped a half circle, landing farther down the river, this time hidden in the marsh.

"Here, some food for the fugitive." He offered her a sandwich, which she declined, and he ate in silence as she examined the world around them. The water splashed against the hull, and small waves crashed on the shore. The river felt soothing, almost maternal, as though the rhythmic wobbling were a rocking lullaby, yet still, it did not conceal its ability to sink and drown her on a whim. Deep layers of transparent clouds shifted above, and Claudia, suspended between air and water, life and death, was reminded of her utter insignificance.

7

Claudia still reveled in yesterday's river adventure. She was getting better at savoring those times when her anxiety retreated for extended periods and had been attempting to prolong them as much as possible. Sometimes, during those periods, she felt so healthy and normal that she began to believe a cure was possible. Her senses would become sharper and her mind more inquisitive, and at times, when she felt a touch of hunger, she could derive some pleasure from eating a simple meal. This nourishment, in turn, would bring her greater clarity, allowing her to feel like her former lively self. She made more effort today when dressing, putting on a simple cream-colored blouse and a pair of black trousers.

She browsed the downstairs library for maps of the river, wanting to compare modern geography with the old courses of the waterway. Had Watershed Island changed its shape over time? How many other islands were nearby? Which channels were manmade and when had they been dug? How far were they from the ocean? How large was the estuary, and how long would it take to navigate there?

She couldn't find any area maps but came across an atlas of pre-Columbian cartography. The deformed and exaggerated shapes of the European, Asian, and African continents gave the impression of mythical, made-up lands. Some of them depicted exotic animals and alien peoples. Such a fantastic array of flavors and excitement had awaited ancient explorers. Some maps described the earth as flat; others suggested a sphere. On one, Claudia saw the fabled Atlantis, and others omitted both American continents, concentrating only on the Eurasian landmass. Claudia thought about the hundreds of previous generations who had lived their entire lives in abject ignorance. They accepted the view of the world presented to them without questioning it, one in which they functioned and flourished. After all, the merchants used the ancient trading routes marked on the historical drawings. The spices, silk, gold, and timber were tangible proofs the maps were an accurate representation of reality. The rivers were there, and so were the oceans, the mountains, and the deserts. And yet, the true perception of reality eluded them.

"Good morning, Claudia. Do you have a minute to chat?" Richard stood in the doorway, smiling warmly.

"Of course," she replied, closing the atlas and pursing her lips. She hadn't been looking for company, but she would oblige him.

"In my office, please." He escorted her elegantly, and she found herself sitting on the brown leather sofa across from his desk, while he chose one of the armchairs.

"Have you had a chance to explore the island yet? The forest is full of wonders. I don't have the time myself, but I hear the blackberries are exceptional." He glowed with excitement.

"Yes, I took a walk yesterday. The island is a bit larger than I expected. And the fall seems to be coming earlier this year?" Claudia's conversation skills were a bit smoother this time around.

"Yes, yes, it is." Richard agreed wholeheartedly. "How is your cello sonata coming along?" He adjusted a gold pin on his tie.

"It's going well. I'm working on the structure and some thematic ideas," Claudia lied flawlessly.

"I see." He looked away and out the window, and then suddenly smacked both of his knees in excitement.

"Claudia, I have an interesting proposition for you." He paused for a moment as she looked at him curiously. "How would you like to write a symphony?"

Oh, not that again! She had thought the topic was closed.

"Well, we already talked about it. I stated my intentions and—"

"I know, I know," he interrupted, "but let me present my idea. I think you might find it attractive."

She forced her shut lips into a tight smile and nodded.

"You see, my daughter, Adrienne, is looking for a symphony right now."

"Do you mean to program it on a concert?"

"Yes." He nodded firmly. "I mean, no. Not exactly." He cleared his throat, stretching the side of his neck. "She needs to write a symphony for the Helmer-Hoffmann Competition."

Claudia didn't follow. A wrinkle on her forehead betrayed her.

"You see," he continued, "Adrienne's career has really taken off in the last two years. She is completing her residency at the Ravena Philharmonic; she just received a commission from the Bornholm Sinfonietta and a contract from Platinova Records."

Claudia still didn't follow.

"Oh, Claudia, let me spell it out for you: She doesn't have the time to write a symphony," he said impatiently. "She simply has too much on her plate at the moment. The Helmer-Hoffmann Competition is only held once every three years and, as you very well know, it is a monumental stepping stone in a composer's career. She can't miss it. It will be a powerful building block on her resume."

Claudia's synapses were jolted by a sudden burst of electricity. *So this is Adrienne Holbert.* The

Adrienne Holbert, a graduate of the New England School of Modern Arts and the New Century University, who received the Mirelli Fellowship for a year of study in Italy? The same Adrienne Holbert who was selected the Most Promising Young Composer of the Year by Sonoritica Magazine*? The Adrienne Holbert who received a commission from the Brostovsky Ballet? Adrienne Holbert wants* me *to write a symphony for* her*?*

"But why me?" Claudia laughed. The entire situation was surreal. She grabbed the decorative pillow beside her and pressed it against her thigh.

"You are very capable, Claudia. I have seen your orchestral writing. Granted, you have only written short pieces, but you are certainly ready to write a symphony." Richard looked at her earnestly.

"Yes, but isn't that unethical or even illegal?" She lowered her voice and leaned in.

"Claudia, we are both adults here. We both know how very competitive the music world can be. One must be aggressive in pursuing one's career goals." He looked away. A small wrinkle appeared in the middle of his forehead. "Adrienne, of course, is very talented, more than capable of writing her own symphony, but we are talking strategic planning within a very constrictive timeframe." He pronounced every word with exemplary clarity. "If it wasn't for all the other fantastic opportunities she could not pass up,"—he waved his hands, as if juggling marble balls—"she would be certainly writing it herself."

Claudia's congenial smile gradually transformed into a grimace of bewilderment. She didn't know how to steer the conversation without angering Richard or saying something she would later regret.

"But I also believe," he continued, "that this project could greatly benefit you. First of all,"—his hands held an imaginary box—"you would gain a valuable experience composing a major work, and secondly,"—the box moved to the other side—"you would be financially compensated for your time and effort. I'm sure a doctoral assistant would welcome a healthy infusion of substantial resources, wouldn't you agree?"

Was this a rhetorical question? Claudia calculated all the variables in her mind. She weighed Richard's motives, those of his daughter's, her own.

"But my compositional style is very different from Adrienne's. I don't think it would be what she's looking for." Claudia played along, curious how far she could take it and what valuable information she could glean.

"I don't know what you young people write these days. In my time, we had the last of the serialists, some minimalists, and lots of modern incoherent gibberish." He leaned back into his chair but allowed his fingers to play atop the shiny desk. "Nowadays, I see random gobbledygook is still in style. No one really knows how to distinguish one piece from another. I don't think it matters all that much what you come up with. I'm not sure the symphony would even be performed. It's more of an honorary award, based on the resume, provenance, and the pedigree of the composer. You know the system." He waved off the thought.

Yes, she was very familiar with the system. She was a part of it. It didn't matter what she knew. It mattered where she went to school. It didn't matter what she wrote in a scholastic paper. It mattered at which conference the paper was presented.

"Suppose I did write it. What makes you think my symphony would win the competition?" Claudia tested the feasibility of Richard's plan, dealing a blow where it appeared most improbable.

"Claudia, Claudia, you are so innocent!" A full smile returned to his face. "I admire your worldview. I wish more people shared your sentiments. Adrienne has already won. It is more or less a formality." His teeth were spaced evenly, no doubt a set of costly veneers.

Claudia stared coldly ahead. She stood up slowly, trying to retain her composure, to remain professional and cordial. She believed one should never burn any bridges or give binary answers. She certainly wasn't about to commit to this scam, but neither would she storm out like some idealistic schoolgirl. She was an adult, a player—apparently a valuable one. She would merely put the topic on hold.

"Richard, I thank you for considering me for

this project. I will have to think about it. Let me get back to you," she said slowly.

"Absolutely, absolutely," said Richard. "Yes, this is a large undertaking and a serious decision. I don't want to pressure you in any way. This is something you must feel comfortable with. But also, please remember you now have less than six weeks here at Watershed and the competition deadline is three months away."

Claudia nodded and strode out of the office, wrapping her forearms around her stomach.

8

When Claudia returned to the library, she heard Richard step out of his office and leave the villa. The truck engine started up shortly and she concluded he must be returning to the mainland. She resumed her cartography study but found she could no longer concentrate. She closed the atlas and held it close to her chest.

Should she call someone? What would she say? That Adrienne Holbert wants her, Claudia Morton from Grayland State, to compose a winning symphony? Who would believe her? And it wasn't as if she was being forced or blackmailed or that she was in any danger. She was not frightened.

She wasn't about to talk to any of her fellow composers, either. They all had private dealings with all kinds of ensembles and grants organizations. One never knew how projects were awarded or who was commissioned for what favor and to whom. Was she now being initiated into this world of back-room politics? Did she have something to bring to the table, something to trade? For what exactly? Richard had mentioned payment, although he didn't specify the amount. It wouldn't take much to make a significant difference in Claudia's budget, but just how much exactly, before she would seriously consider it?

She heard about rigged ice skating competitions, but somehow never imagined it in her own field. Was it illegal? Punishable by federal law, like fraud? Or something lesser, like plagiarism at a university? Would she be discovered, fired, stripped of her degrees, expelled from the school, forbidden to publish or to teach? She stood and began to pace the room, away from the armchairs and the bookshelves, toward the grand piano and back again.

Although she had not met Richard before, she vaguely recalled hearing about Ann Holbert, the director of the Global Arts Vision Foundation, who chaired the grants division. Could she be Richard's wife, sister? Could Claudia's alliance with them open up doors to that level of arts funding, propel her to circles she had only ever read about in magazines or liner notes of recordings? Could she get letters of recommendation and the coveted tenure track at a desirable university? Could the trajectory of her life depend on this single decision—to sell her music and remain silent? If she agreed, she would, in practical terms, be using her music to earn her living. Her own music would finally be the currency of her trade. And what was dishonest in that?

All these thoughts knotted themselves in her

skull. She couldn't begin to untie the tangle, to make any sense of it. She wished she could talk to someone, to pick their brains and to help her see the situation objectively.

The house was quiet and felt deserted, but as she left the library, she spotted Victor in the art studio. He was sitting hunched over his laptop, which he had placed on a makeshift desk constructed from a side table and a few photography albums. Diego's paints were scattered on the worktable and the floor, and his canvases and sheets of watercolor paper were propped against the bookcase and the wall.

"How's the novel coming?" Claudia asked, peering through the doorway.

"It's going well. Quite well," he answered, still hunched, typing without taking his eyes off the screen.

Claudia knew better than to disturb an artist in the flow of his craft, but since the door of the studio was wide open and she was dying to talk to someone, she walked in quietly.

"So, who's the murderer?" she persisted.

"There is no murderer. I don't like to use physical force unless I absolutely have to. I prefer to send my characters on emotional roller coasters." Not a hint of a smile; he was still immersed in his writing.

Tell me about it, she yearned to say, but instead chose, "How do you send them there?" She sat down in the chair next to his.

He pulled himself from the screen to face her and sighed.

"Well, I just finished writing a pleasant intro and threw the first curveball into the plot."

"Is this—what was it?—a psychological thriller? Is that your favorite genre?" she asked.

"No, I've written all kinds of things. I enjoy the variety." He crossed his legs and arms in anticipation of a more involved conversation.

"Have you ever . . . I mean, do you think . . ." She paused, bringing her fingers together. "Have you ever written something for someone else?" She looked intently into his eyes. They were neither blue nor green, just the color of purity and transparency.

"What do you mean? Like a love poem?"

She blushed and looked away.

"No, I mean, have you written something that you let another person pass off as their own? Let them pretend they wrote it?"

Victor smiled and looked toward the window, then back at her again.

"Of course. In high school, I wrote a lot of papers for other students. I had my own side business going for a while. It was so profitable, I thought I would have to start a franchise. Then in grad school,"—he squinted at the ceiling—"there may have been instances of certain,"—he swallowed loudly—"master's theses being produced. Allegedly."

"But professionally? For example, writing for another writer?"

"Like ghostwriting?"

"Precisely!" She clapped her hands in excitement.

"Ah! Yes, of course. I wrote the autobiography of Stephen Derenson."

"The golf player?" she exclaimed.

"That's the one," he nodded.

"But were you credited for it? Did your name appear on the book cover? That's what usually happens, isn't it? So-and-so author in capital letters with so-and-so author in smaller letters at the bottom?"

"Yes, but not in my case. I didn't want it." Grimacing, Victor looked at his hands.

"You didn't?"

"I'm a novelist. Why would I want my name attached to an autobiography of some golfer?"

Claudia thought for a moment. That made sense to her.

"He paid me well, so it all worked out," he added.

"But what if you wrote a novel—a very good one—and someone asked you to give it to them, to sell your authorship, allowing them to take full credit for it?" Claudia asked, with growing agitation.

"That, my friend, is called work-for-hire. It

happens all the time. You have skills, you get hired, you do your job, you exit, you cash the check." He shrugged.

"But what about your intellectual property?"

"There is no property. You just sold your property. You made a calculated transaction." Rubbing his hands together, he emphasized every word.

"And your soul? Your talent? I don't know, your inspiration?" she asked.

"Ah! Here lies the pressure point. You are emotionally attached to your property." He wagged his index finger at her. "You think your intellectual property equals your soul, that you are selling yourself."

"Yes, yes, that's right! That's what it feels like!" She stood up, cupping her hands around her cheeks. "I can't have someone else take credit for my work and allow them to reap the benefits while I remain in the shadows. I can't let them use the fruits of my creative labor, my artistic essence!"

Victor looked at her calmly, waiting for her to finish. She felt foolish for spilling her emotions so easily.

"Are you asking my advice on a situation in which you may or may not have presently found yourself?"

"I guess so. I just need someone to bounce this off of." She dropped back into her chair.

"Someone off whom to bounce," he corrected

her, crinkling his nose and poking her upper arm.

"Shut up!" She slapped his hand, and they both laughed in camaraderie.

"Listen, Claudia, I don't know what to tell you. People ghostwrite, they apprentice, they assist—they do whatever advances their careers in the long run. If it helps you and you can live with it, then you should do it." He looked at her intently with those bright, transparent, all-seeing eyes.

"That's the problem. I'm not sure I can live with it. Theoretically, it all makes perfect sense, but I don't think I'm cut out for it." She lowered her gaze and shook her head.

Claudia returned to her room where she looked out into the courtyard. The forest remained as steadfast and calm as before. It was grounding, centering. It did not judge her yet brought truth and clarity into every thought. Claudia had failed to mention to Victor the issue of the corrupt competition. This point was what ultimately troubled her the most: the idea that she would participate in deception and that, in the end, her music wouldn't even matter.

She pulled out a piece of paper and her fountain pen and wrote a concise note:

Richard,
Thank you, but I will pass.
Claudia

9

In the afternoon, Claudia returned to the library. No longer interested in the ancient maps, she browsed the music section instead. She was impressed by the extensive collection of miniature orchestral scores: symphonies of Beethoven, Bruckner, Tchaikovsky, Honegger, Strauss, Brahms, Carter, Harris, Barber, editions unknown to her of Mozart's piano concertos, Bach's oratorios, and Haydn's string quartets. There was an entire shelf of chamber music, mostly for strings in various combinations, but also with piano, clarinet, or flute. Poulenc, Milhaud, Prokofiev, Stravinsky—the staples of the early twentieth century—and many more she has never come across: a piano trio by Lalo Molnár, a flute sonata by Vera Linardi, string quartets of Herbert Anders, or woodwind quintets of Witold Kuleczyński.

She took a few of the unfamiliar scores and began to read them, silently mouthing their melodic lines. An avid sight-reader and an experienced orchestrator, Claudia was able to hear the composers' intentions without the aid of any instruments; nevertheless, she took the scores to the grand piano and began to play. Harmonies quite different from anything she herself had ever composed amused her. She took pleasure in flipping at random through the music and pulling fragments of long passages to get a sense of the full piece. After she had gone similarly through several more scores, she gathered them and returned them to the shelf. Another collection beckoned. These were larger orchestral scores written by hand. One for a chamber orchestra with only a few woodwinds and no percussion, and another one entitled *Iphigenia*, with a gigantic orchestral ensemble, choir, and soloists. Its penmanship was exquisite. She promised herself she would return later to examine it in depth.

As she straightened the scores on the shelf, a patterned black notebook caught her eye. Inside, rows of flawless cursive, like strings of curled ribbons, neatly filled the pages. The hard cover and the paper sheets were slightly yellowed with age but remained well preserved and were kept together by the securely sewn binding. At first glance, Claudia thought these were student notes, but upon closer inspection, she realized she held an old diary. Ordinarily, she would feel uneasy about encroaching upon someone else's secrets, but this notebook looked like an antique store find. A historical artifact? A musician's diary? A composer's journal? She sat down and began to read.

April 12, 1965

Spring is warmer than usual this year, a nice change from the dreary winter we have had to endure. I so missed the outings with the ladies from the Central Park Conservancy. Ever since I have helped to organize the last season's charity concert, there has been a talk of me becoming the Society's president for the next three-year term. Is it the right thing for me to pursue? I have made peace with the fact that motherhood has thus far eluded me and is now highly improbable. Perhaps it is the right time to devote my life to public service and give of myself in the ways in which I am gifted. I certainly have had the foretaste of public life by Herbert's side, all throughout his teaching and composing years. But now, I feel I must branch out on my own, with initiatives beyond music, and maybe even beyond the Park Conservancy.

Herbert was severely overworked this academic year, and I fear the strain of the increasing responsibilities will intrude on our travel plans in the summer. I was, of course, overjoyed and immensely proud when Herbert was commissioned by the Metropolitan Opera to compose a major production for the opening of the new opera house at Lincoln Center, but now that he has begun the work, I can see how involved and complicated this project will be. Is it wrong of me to think of charity and service outside of the home when my husband requires my full devotion and support during such an intense time? I try to be there for him in all the ways I know how, but without any musical training, I am not truly able to assist him or even to understand his needs.

As soon as Nadia Boulanger heard of the commission, she sent a congratulatory letter to Herbert, as any proud teacher would to her student. Herbert always speaks so very fondly of their time in Paris, still crediting her for everything he knows about music. I would think it an exaggeration, except that I hear of endless throngs of students who insist on studying with her year after year.

It was Nadia's idea to recommend Rita to us, to help Herbert with orchestrating the work, and how grateful we are for her. Rita, who was once Nadia's student herself, knows the particular shorthand Herbert employs in his creative process and, as I see from across the hallway, is able to read his mind with ease. Hats off to anyone who can decipher Herbert's handwriting. I see her in his study, hunched over stacks of the manuscript, turning piano sketches into multiple layers of orchestral passages. The woman is working her youth away, but she tells me it is an honor to learn from Herbert.

I went for a walk around 39th Street and began feeling all nostalgic about the Metropolitan Opera House's big move. We have seen countless productions there and have the fondest memories of the auditorium. The magnificent staging of Turandot, Arabella, The Rake's Progress, Elektra, Wozzeck.

In everyday life, I loathe gaudiness, preferring self-restraint and simplicity, but when it comes to opera, the larger the spectacle, the better. Just sitting inside that theater, looking at the reliefs on the proscenium, the ceiling, and the balconies, basking in that shimmer of the starburst chandelier and the gold damask stage curtains—it always made me giddy with excitement. The acoustics of the building are as good as in any first-class performance space. . . .

But the artists have suffered long enough in that cramped, stuffy backstage. The acrobatics the stagehands have had to perform! I heard they sometimes had to leave furniture out on the street during set changes! Well, there will be no such madness at the new location.

Since the twenties, several proposals for new sites have been drafted. They came and went without any progress, but the idea of moving to Lincoln Center finally prevailed. We are told the new building will be the talk of the town for decades to come and the productions will be even more spectacular and daring, as if that is even possible. All the more reason I am so very proud the committee chose Herbert to open the first season in the new building. May his music resound there and reverberate for generations to come!

Vocalizations coming from the art studio across the hallway startled Claudia. Stephanie was warming up her vocal cords by gliding to the top of her register, performing acrobatics typical of coloratura sopranos. She sounded like a wounded animal.

Though there were many diary pages left unread, Claudia needed a break. She pushed the notebook back into its spot on the shelf, noting it was next to a dictionary, in order to mark it for later retrieval. She began heading toward the stairs to return to her room when Stephanie called out to her.

"I'm sorry, I didn't realize you were down here. Did my singing bother you?" She looked genuinely concerned. She touched Claudia's arm.

"No, it's fine," Claudia answered quickly. It wasn't fine at all. It was disruptive and annoying, but she was prepared to let it go.

"I'll move to the library, and I'll close the door this time. I like to practice with the piano, and I hope it won't disturb you up in your room." Stephanie was already taking tiny subservient steps, pointing to the library door.

"I'm sure it will be fine," Claudia said, but didn't believe it.

When she returned upstairs, she moved the desk away from the side wall and pushed it to face the window. Looking outdoors was more inspiring than staring at the dark wood paneling. She stretched out her sheets of manuscript paper on the tabletop and reached for some graph paper. From a fabric pouch, she pulled several pencils of various hardness and two architect-grade erasers. She smoothed the paper with her hand, back and forth, as if trying to appease it. She moved to the graph paper and proceeded to draw a diagram, filling it with various shapes decipherable only to herself.

Loud laughter from the courtyard interrupted

the flow of her thoughts. Claudia peered out the window to catch a glimpse of Diego's back at the edge of the bench on the veranda. Presumably, he attempted to sketch Stephanie, since every few seconds he scolded her, "Stop wiggling, you ferret!" or "Sit still, woman!" Stephanie then began to run around, screeching, "Stop it!" and "Get away!" and "No!" as Diego dropped his sketchbook and ran after her, trying to catch her. She shrieked each time he got close, but at the last moment she managed to evade his grasp. They kept shouting, until, finally, he caught her by the hips and lifted her off the ground. He draped her over his shoulder like a hunter would his game, and her dark hair cascaded down past his waist. He slapped her butt, causing her to both scream and giggle at the same time. The abrupt movements mussed his T-shirt, exposing a swath of his fat, hairy stomach.

They reminded Claudia of her more infantile students back at the university. She buried her face in her hands, sighing loudly. Apparently, she hadn't traveled far enough to escape them. When she looked up, the couple were running together, hand in hand, into the forest, laughing and cavorting like schoolchildren during a recess. Claudia stared into the canopies of the trees, looking for something, anything—*anything*—other than what was in front of her.

10

Claudia's dreams were often intense and exhausting. Lately, her mind had been invaded by various three-dimensional shapes. In one, a gigantic block floated steadily toward her, intending to squash her. But it cracked in slow motion, and before it had a chance to reach her, it shattered into small particles that began to dance like an enraged colony of bees. They moved in synchrony, yet, as a whole, remained flexible and pliable. Claudia was able, with her thoughts, without issuing them verbal commands, to control their movements and formations.

In another dream, red, purple, and blue balls rolled down a tilted shelf. Before they fell to the ground, Claudia caught them with the power of her concentration, sorting them by color. Each color then followed its own course, as strings of balls wove themselves loosely like spaghetti, or more tightly like braids, finally to abandon any purpose and order in favor of becoming a hovering mesh of scattered pixels.

Upon waking, she was often surprised to find herself on this side of reality, having just left behind the other, no less tangible and grueling than the present. She usually experienced then not so much a headache as a pressure and a tightness in her temples. She dreaded falling asleep again, in fear that the tiring cycle would continue.

And so it was this morning in bed when, with the grace of a rag doll and squinting from the blinding light pouring in through the window, she propped herself up on her elbows to gather her bearings. The sun was higher and clearer than usual. She must have overslept. She reached for her nightstand to locate her watch when, in the corner of her eye, a dark figure moved. Jolting upright, she reflexively curled herself against the headboard, frantically pulling the comforter over her naked body. Her feet kept kicking and slipping down the sheets as she tried to assume the optimal defensive position.

"Good morning, *Venus*," Diego greeted her softly. He sat in a chair at the foot of the bed, a large sheet of paper on cardboard propped against his bent knee. He scratched at it with a thick graphite pencil.

"What the hell are you doing here, you pervert? Get out!" Claudia screamed, tightening the bedding around her torso, smoothing it on the side with her hand, strengthening her new fortress. She instinctively reached for her pubic area under the cover, checking for damage. Had she been assaulted? Raped? She didn't feel achy or soiled. She squeezed her thighs, shuddering at the thought.

"Relax, *Ariadne*. You were a perfect model. If you could only see the way this light hits the bed in the morning." Diego pointed to the window. "Goya's *Nude Maja*—that's what you were. I had to draw you or I would never forgive myself." He set the paper on the floor next to him, then stood up.

Claudia cowered, pulling the covers even tighter to her chest. She was painfully aware of her small, girlish breasts and her thin, bony frame. "How did you get in here?" She remembered there was no lock on the door. She tried to brush her hair from her cheeks. "What happened? Did we . . . ? I don't remember last night." Her voice shook.

"Oh, don't be so melodramatic. You had a few beers and went to bed a little tipsy. I came to check on you this morning because you were asleep for so long." He walked toward the window, farther away from her, and leaned against the wooden casing. "When I came in and saw you, *Sleeping Endymion*, I went to get my pencils and had to commit you to paper. There was no debating it."

"I find it highly, highly inappropriate!" Claudia was clinging to the headboard, shaking. She tried to define what had happened, to categorize it: trespassing? Sexual harassment? Assault? And why was she naked? Had she undressed herself last night? Had she been completely inebriated? Did he help her to bed? Did he take off her clothes? Her blouse, trousers, and undergarments were draped neatly over the side of the armchair.

"Dear *Ophelia*, if we only did what was highly appropriate, we would still paint pineapples and persimmons on silver trays." He sounded disappointed. He sighed, bent to gather a dozen scattered paper panels from the floor, and then walked out of the room.

Claudia remained in bed, unable to move. She should make an official complaint. What was the chain of command here? She would talk to Richard. Richard? Please, not him again. Ms. Bertha? No, what could she possibly do? Someone from the Foundation. She would report a hostile environment. That's right. Hostility, invasion of privacy, harassment, and bullying. And lewd, inappropriate comments. She wasn't quite sure about the technicality of the last charge.

A soft knock on the door startled her.

"Claudia, dear," Ms. Bertha called softly, "I brought you breakfast. You've been sleeping for a very long time. I just want to make sure you are all right."

Claudia stood quickly, wrapped a sheet around herself, and opened the door.

"Rough night, dear?" Ms. Bertha asked, peering in.

"Yes. Thank you for thinking of me." Claudia opened the door wider.

"I'll just put the tray here on your desk." Ms. Bertha strode resolutely toward the window and set the clanking dishes on the table. "Honestly, I don't know how you artists stay alive." She turned to face Claudia and wrapped her fingers in a prayerful lament. "You must eat something, honey. You are all skin and bones. Forgive me for saying it, but you need some real food."

The tray contained two boiled eggs, two strips of bacon, a piece of toast with a dish of jam, orange juice, and coffee. The woman's kindness touched Claudia.

"Thank you so much, Ms. Bertha. You are an angel."

"Have some food, dear." The woman sounded mildly impatient, like a grandmother scolding her granddaughter. She walked past Claudia, patted her forearm, and left without waiting for a reply, closing the door behind her.

Claudia sat by the desk, still wrapped in her sheets, staring numbly into the space in front of her. This place wasn't going to work out after all. She could not rest here. Even if she tried to work, she wouldn't be able to concentrate. First this issue with Richard, then Stephanie, and now this pervert Diego. Too many things were causing her stress and anxiety. When she reached for the coffee cup, her hands shook. She felt dizzy and short of breath again. The dull pain in her stomach radiated out with its familiar warmth into her other organs. There was no use in prolonging this experiment. She would leave, and she would leave today.

She crunched down her toast with new resolve and then removed the tray from the desk, placing it on the nightstand. She propped the desk against the door to barricade herself in. She unwrapped her sheet tunic and took a quick shower. Brushed her teeth and spruced up her hair but didn't put on any makeup. The sooner she could be gone, the better. She dressed quickly and shoved the rest of her clothes into her suitcase, gathered her notebooks, her laptop, and her manuscript papers. With a swift push of the desk away from the door, she was on her way down the stairs and swiftly maneuvering with her luggage out through the front door.

"Are you leaving us?" Victor rose from the bench on the veranda with a cup of coffee in his hand. He looked surprised.

"Yes, I'm afraid I am," Claudia answered without looking at him.

"Emergency at home?" he prodded.

"No, nothing like that. I just need to leave." She sounded short with him, impatient.

"Is there anything I can do for you?" He took half a step toward her.

"No." She backed away. "There is nothing to be done. This place is not what I imagined. I think I will only be wasting my time here." Her eyes were watering, and she readjusted her grip on the black portfolio and her laptop bag.

"But you barely just got here. You have to give yourself some time to settle in. Where are you going to write your sonata?" Victor pleaded.

"I couldn't care less about the sonata—or about writing anything at all!" she barked with an honesty of someone who has been pushed over the edge. "I can't be here. I just can't do it. I can't do it anymore!" She was on the verge of tears. Not tears of sorrow or regret, but tears of humiliation and powerlessness. The kind of tears one is ashamed to cry and utterly helpless to stop. She could not hold them back any longer. "I was hoping to find inspiration and some spark here, but I see this place is impossible," she continued. "This is a sick and abusive environment." She pointed angrily at the villa. She desperately tried to control herself while shuffling her belongings and balancing the suitcase.

Victor looked patiently at her, allowing her to finish the outburst; he seemed to understand.

"Listen, Claudia," he spoke quietly and evenly. "I don't know what your game plan is here, but all I've seen you do these past three days is fumble around. Are you here to work, or are you here on some lazy-ass vacation?" He moved closer, speaking directly at her, leaning in. "It's cute that you want to find your glittery sparks, your soul, your artistic essence, and whatnot, but I don't think you understand why professionals come to Watershed." He stared at her, not backing away.

"That's a little harsh and condescending, don't you think? I am a professional, and I certainly resent your mansplaining." But Claudia could not compete with his stern gaze, and she looked away.

"My apologies for trying to bring you to your senses." He rolled his eyes and raised his arms in capitulation.

Claudia ran down the veranda steps into the gravel courtyard.

"Where are you going?" Victor shouted after her.

She marched quickly toward the dock. "Away from this sick place!"

"The ferry isn't running today!" Victor called from the porch.

She stopped in her tracks.

"It only runs on Tuesdays and Fridays." He laughed out loud, and then retreated into the villa, leaving her to fend for herself.

Her knees collapsed, and she dropped onto her suitcase. She shoved away her portfolio and laptop bag, and they landed on the sandy pathway, gathering scuffs and dirt.

"Fuck! Shit! Fuck this shit!" she raged, kicking her heels in the gravel, puffing up clouds of dust.

11

Victor's assessment had been very observant and calculated. Claudia hated him for it. She knew writers to be perceptive and analytical, but had imagined them as more sympathetic, ambiguous, impartial. She wondered about his novels and his writing style. No doubt he churned out some dry crime procedurals. But, of course, he was right. Dead on. Yes, she was fumbling around. No, she hadn't suspected it was so obvious to the others.

She returned to her room and reluctantly unpacked. The ferry would be here in a couple of days and she could always leave then, but for now, somehow, she had to make it through the rest of this day. One way or another, she had to get out of the villa. The house confined her, made her feel claustrophobic, imprisoned.

She decided to go in search of blackberries in the woods, as good a reason as any other. The river was quiet, but the insects were buzzing all around and the wind combed the tall grasses. A steady procession of disciplined ants crossed the path at her feet. Heading down the hill, she recognized the path she had taken with Gabriel earlier. She followed it all the way to the small dock. There was no sign of him or his boat, or anyone else for that matter. Why was she here? She wasn't looking for him. Why would she? The most he could do for her was give her a ride to the mainland. Yes, maybe that was it. She sat on the pier and gazed into the water. At the bottom, brown and gold gravel sparkled in the afternoon sun. The weathered wooden planks of the dock felt rough under her fingers.

She recalled how indifferent she had been the time she was with him, and how dramatically her mood had shifted in just the last forty-eight hours—and not for the better. She preferred feeling numb to emotional upheaval. She thought about her derailed life, which she was no longer able to control or to understand. She was hopeless, impotent.

Was Victor right? Was she too emotional? Could she become more objective, professional, pragmatic, detached? What if she wrote music no matter what? Put aside all feelings, emotions, drama, and engineer the bloody thing, the way one would design a building or a highway. She had to give it a try. What did she have to lose? An afternoon and a piece of paper?

The next day she woke early and after cleaning up and removing her nightly barricade from the door (she wasn't taking any chances), she set to work. She decided to attempt the cello sonata after all. She had no desire and no inspiration to compose; she didn't hear any music in her head, nor did she have any ideas to develop. Nevertheless, she kept doodling with her pencil on the graph paper. She remembered the classic shape of the traditional sonata form. She would structure her composition similarly, perhaps altering it slightly to suit her needs. She jotted down a few melodic lines, then copied them in inversion and retrograde. Expanding certain intervals modified the new melodies but kept their cohesion with the originals. She knew the cello's registers, their strengths and weaknesses, their timbres, and their harmonic series. She understood instinctively which themes would be best suited for each. She worked slowly and methodically.

She took a short break for lunch, hoping she wouldn't have to interact with anyone in the kitchen. Thankfully, the entire house was deserted. The doors to the painting studio and the dining room were shut. She moved on tiptoe, closing the kitchen door behind her before setting out her dishes and reheating the food.

She worked in earnest that entire afternoon and was surprised to find she had lost track of time for a couple of hours. It felt good. At least now she could honestly say she did have early sketches of the sonata and was making some progress. Even if the music was worthless, she had a bottom off which to push upward.

A knock on her door interrupted her thoughts.

"Claudia, do you mind if we talk?" Stephanie

was already finding her way in.

Claudia reluctantly pointed her to the armchair, but she sat on the edge of the bed instead.

"I want to apologize for Diego," she said with a deep sigh.

"It's not for you to apologize for him," Claudia said, looking at her sternly.

"I know, but I feel like I need to explain. You see, he is very driven and can be brash and forceful sometimes, but he would never hurt you. It's just that he is obsessed with his art." She made herself more comfortable on the bed and leaned against the headboard.

"I gathered that much," Claudia said.

"Please don't be upset about him barging into your room the way he did. He can be clueless and rude. Are you feeling okay?"

She seemed genuine, if somewhat dramatic, but Claudia certainly wasn't about to open up to this schoolgirl. She wanted to get rid of her quickly.

"I'll be fine. I just got a little ruffled. He better not try it again." She twisted back toward the desk, hoping the girl would get the hint and leave her to continue her work.

"Oh, no, he won't," Stephanie assured her, fervently. "He might ask you to pose for him, though. Fully clothed, I mean. He has been after me all this time." She rolled her eyes and waved her hand. "He's wearing me out with all this posing and sitting still for hours on end."

No doubt in the nude, Claudia thought. The girl's physique was clearly lifted out of a Rubens painting.

"Listen, Claudia, I think perhaps there is a reason why we have found ourselves on this island together, you know? Kind of like destiny?" She leaned forward, closer to Claudia.

Here we go. The Girl Scout Sisterhood of Watershed. God help us. Claudia was about to sigh loudly but held her breath.

"I think that we can help each other here," Stephanie went on, and Claudia struggled to keep her composure. "I want to tell you something that may seem a little strange, but please bear with me." She paused, as if to make sure Claudia was receptive.

Claudia, now very impatient, hoped Stephanie would finally get to the point.

"I want to be a symphony."

And I want to be a forest, thought Claudia. *What is this? Some kind of newspeak of the younger generation?*

"I'm not good with words. I know this sounds weird, but please hear me out," Stephanie continued. "I know who I am, deep down. People don't get me. Diego doesn't understand me." She looked away, biting her nails. "He wants me to be a painting, and I have tried, I went along with it, but I'm just not cut out for it. As soon as I met you,"—she turned to Claudia again with a radiant smile—"I just felt this immediate connection, you know? Like, this revelation. And I just know that you are the right person to help me."

Claudia was baffled but determined to bring this bizarre conversation to its conclusion.

"Stephanie, I've heard you sing. If you are to be anything, you should be an opera. Girl, with your coloratura range, you would be throwing your talent away if you were anything else." Claudia thought her joke was witty and lighthearted, but Stephanie was visibly upset and disappointed.

"I have tried to be that, but it's not who I am meant to be. I never thought it would be so hard to convince others—especially a composer like yourself."

Claudia was becoming more confused with each sentence. She stood up and rested her hands on the back of her chair. She then pushed up her sleeves and pulled them down again. She opened her mouth to form a response but was only able to exhale.

Stephanie persisted. "Do you know what it's like to be stuck in a place where you have absolutely no hope of reaching your full potential? To be relegated to some menial existence, to live in a body that doesn't represent your soul?"

Yes, Claudia knew that firsthand, but where was this conversation headed and what was the meaning of this allegory the girl was spinning?

"Richard is right," Stephanie began to cry. "You are more than capable of writing a symphony. You are wasting your time composing this cello sonata of yours. You may not want to write music for Adrienne, but you could compose it for yourself."

"What have you heard about Richard and Adrienne?" Claudia was alarmed. She grabbed Stephanie's arm. "Have you talked to him? What did he tell you?"

"I didn't have to talk to him. I know what's going on in this villa." Tears rolled down her silky, doll-like cheeks.

"I don't understand what it is that you want from me. You'll have to speak more clearly." Claudia would get to the bottom of it. She sat on the edge of the bed, facing Stephanie.

"You are an artist, a composer, and you don't understand when I speak plainly? I am begging you to write the symphony. I am asking you to write me!" Stephanie shouted, leaping upright.

The girl was clearly deranged. She was in some kind of delusional state. She sobbed, gasping for air. Claudia stood, too, and patted her gently on the shoulder. She tried to appease her but had no clue where to begin. Perhaps, if she could get Stephanie out of her room and into Diego's care, he would know how to handle her.

Claudia was reminded of a freshman student in her class two years ago. She had been disruptive during lectures and kept bursting out in song. Other students thought it hilarious at first, but when her behavior continued, Claudia was forced to call security to escort her out of the building. The dean later informed her the girl had been committed to a mental institution.

Alarmed, Claudia carefully studied Stephanie's face. Was this something stress-related, or maybe something more serious? Claudia didn't know anything about her, other than what Stephanie had told her that very first evening.

"Stephanie, please don't be upset. We'll figure this out." She held the girl's hand, rubbing it between her palms. "Please get a hold of yourself. Do you want me to call Diego?"

"No, I'll go now." But she continued sobbing. "Tell me you will think about what I said. It's very important."

"Yes, of course," Claudia promised her, walking her to the door.

Of course, she would not only think about it, she would naturally obsess over it. She would try to figure out how to get Stephanie some help, how to help her own self, and how to finally escape this crazed island, once and for all.

12

Pillow-top mattress or no, silence or none, Claudia could not sleep the entire night. Her mind would not let her rest but remained in a continuous state of alarm. She was no longer afraid of Diego—she had forgotten to barricade herself in—but now was obsessing over her conversation with Stephanie. There must be some procedure to follow here. She tried to remember all her new teacher orientations and sensitivity training sessions at the university. What to do during a fire, what to do during a shooting, how to handle combative parents, how to deal with entitled students, how to report suicidal or self-harming students, how to recognize potentially dangerous individuals, how to establish boundaries during individual lessons. Still, the only way she thought she could help Stephanie was by talking to Richard or by contacting the Foundation. She didn't feel the situation was dire enough to call the police or the paramedics. The girl didn't seem to be a danger to herself or others.

But then, maybe Claudia was overreacting. So what if the girl wanted to be a symphony? She might be a little over-inspired, wildly imaginative, highly sensitive. Had she not mentioned a desire to branch out from the opera? Was that not how those opera singers were, anyway? Divas, prima donnas, drama queens? Yes, of course, that was it! It was an act. Stephanie was probably performing some kind of a theatrical exercise by trying to elicit an emotional reaction from Claudia. The girl was good, no doubt about it. Claudia had almost fallen for it.

This explanation relieved her partially and she tried to return to sleep, but the early morning light was already peering through the lower tree branches. There was no use staying in bed. Her body temperature was rising, and the comforter became a nuisance.

She rose slowly, taking a moment to observe the trees across the courtyard. Their crowns swayed in the wind and tiny leaves shook in unison. What sounded like a million needles falling against the sheet of the metal roof announced the arrival of rain. The white noise enveloped her room, soothing her worn-out psyche.

She had a couple of hours before she needed to catch the ferry, and she had time to get ready in a leisurely manner. She didn't just feel at peace about her decision to leave—she was energized, relieved. She showered, dressed, tied her hair in a ponytail, and applied some mascara and lipstick. She folded her clothes and placed them neatly inside the suitcase. Then, she headed down to the kitchen for coffee and maybe to find a bite to eat before the journey home. Ms. Bertha was just placing the filter in the coffeemaker.

"Good morning, Ms. Bertha," Claudia greeted her warmly.

"Oh, good morning, dear. Did you sleep well?" Ms. Bertha turned around, smiling.

"Well enough, I suppose. I'm very sorry to tell you I will be leaving the island today." She took a mug from the cupboard, waiting for the coffee to finish brewing.

"So early in your residency? Is there trouble back home?" Ms. Bertha asked with a great deal of concern.

"No, there's no trouble. I simply . . . well, I've had a good time here, and you have been a wonderful host." Claudia reached for a piece of toast from the plate of it on the table. "You certainly have a lovely place, and you opening it to artists the way you do—well, it's just wonderful." Claudia gesticulated with the toast, struggling to find the right words. "But I think I'm more suited to working back at home."

"Of course, Claudia, I understand. I'm sorry you will be passing on this opportunity, but yes, every artist must follow her instinct, and you know what is best for your creative pathway. I will certainly miss having you here." Ms. Bertha looked at her with sorrow. "But how will you get back to the mainland?"

"Isn't the ferry running today?" Claudia asked.

"Ordinarily, yes, but I just received a weather advisory over the radio. A massive storm is headed our way."

Claudia's posture drooped and her jaw went slack.

"When it rains like this, the ferry only goes to Overlook Island, but today, I doubt it will make it even that far."

"What am I supposed to do?" Claudia dropped heavily onto the chair.

"There is nothing to be done but wait for the storm to pass. You can travel next week." Ms. Bertha poured milk into the cream jug.

Claudia was defeated once again. Everything on this island was conspiring against her. She had thought it was just the people, but now even nature was joining in. She wanted to scream but instead only sighed.

She went upstairs and sat aimlessly on the bed, facing the window. This place was cursed or haunted. No, it was downright antagonistic and devious. It wasn't conducive to any creative work. It was a sorry, pathetic, creepy place that happened to draw deranged and unbalanced people, Ms. Bertha excluded.

The rain kept falling gently onto the courtyard and the veranda. Gray clouds floated slowly through the sky, but a sliver of pure cyan gave hope of an imminent clearing. It looked like any common late-summer shower. Perhaps the weather advisory had been overzealous.

She saw Gabriel close and latch the door to the shed, then stride into the courtyard. He was carrying folded tarps under one arm, and with the other, he lifted the collar of his jacket to keep the rain from falling on his neck. He turned toward the main road and proceeded down the hill.

Gabriel, yes, of course! Gabriel would give her a ride to the mainland. She was home free! She jumped up and shoved her manuscript paper into the black portfolio. She struggled with the zipper but managed to make it travel all the way around the seam.

"Gabriel, wait, Gabriel!" she shouted at the window, although it was impossible for him to hear her. She got tangled in her jacket and suitcase but succeeded in getting out through the bedroom door and down the stairs. She carried everything down in one swoop but almost missed the last step. She clumsily made her way through the front entrance and onto the veranda.

"Gabriel!" she shouted, but the rain muted all the other sounds but its own. "My laptop! Where's my laptop?" She realized it was still upstairs and, leaving the luggage behind, she raced up the stairs, two at a time. The laptop bag was still on her desk, but she had left the power cord plugged into the wall. She yanked it out and coiled it quickly, then pushed it into a side pocket.

She ran downstairs again and collected her luggage, then surged into the courtyard. The large, heavy droplets drenched her immediately. She didn't care. She would catch up to Gabriel and make it out of there today—right now. The suitcase twisted her arm with every bump in the gravel road. Its wheels splashed up dark brown mud as they plowed through the ground instead of rolling atop it. Her large portfolio bounced back and forth as she neither walked nor ran but hobbled forward in an awkward sequence of tiny steps.

"Gabriel! Wait!" she shouted, but he was already gone. She came to the smaller road that branched to the left. Which way had he gone? To the ferry dock or to the side pier? There were no fresh footsteps on the ground, only muddy indentations and puddles everywhere. She had a hunch he would be at the small dock and decided to head there. The pathway narrowed, and it became even more difficult to pull the suitcase. She kept pace despite the pain in her shoulders and the incessant rain. She was almost there. She had to get there in time before he left. This was her last chance. She had to make it!

She looked toward the dock, half hidden behind the greenery of the shrubs and tall grasses. He was there. He was still there!

"Gabriel, wait!" she yelled, desperately.

He was in his boat, hunched down and moving things around. As soon as he heard her voice, he looked up, smiling the biggest, happiest smile. She was safe! She beamed back at him and slowed a little, exhausted. When she finally reached the wooden pier, he stepped out of the boat to meet her halfway.

"Oh, thank God! I'm so glad I caught you! Can you please take me to the mainland?" She breathed heavily.

"Are you running away again?" He still smiled warmly, happy to see her, and seemed oblivious to the pouring rain.

"Yes, I am. Officially, this time. Luggage and everything." She looked down at her belongings, clutching them to her sides.

"I'm sorry, Claudia, but I can't take you today." He shook his head and began to unfold one of the tarps.

Her face soured. "Why not?"

"A weather advisory just came in. There's a storm front moving in quickly. It's very dangerous." His expression was stern.

"But I don't mind. I have to get out of here. You don't understand. Please, take me to the mainland," she pleaded, desperately. "It's not that far, is it?" She pointed to the river, as if the mainland were right there, at the stretch of her hand.

"I'm sorry, I can't do that. I could never do anything to endanger you."

He stopped what he was doing and stood there, looking at her with compassion, allowing the rain to flow freely down his brow and the sides of his face. Her jacket was thoroughly soaked, and her hair clung to her cheeks and mouth. She would have brushed it away, but both of her hands were full.

"But you're going, aren't you?" she asked angrily.

"No, I'm not," he replied calmly.

"Then why are you here?" she shouted in an accusatory tone.

"I came to cover the boat with tarp and to tie it down with extra ropes."

Claudia was speechless. She wanted to have the tantrum of all tantrums. She dropped her portfolio and the laptop bag onto the wet dock. She walked away, covering her face and rubbing her eyes. She paced back and forth aimlessly, muttering incoherently to herself. She pulled her hands away. Black mascara streaked down her wrists. She wasn't sure whether she was crying or if it was the rain that flooded her eyelashes. She didn't need a mirror to know she appeared pathetic. She saw it on his face, a look of concern, maybe even of pity. He spoke softly as he reached for her belongings.

"Here, let me help you with these."

13

Panic does not come suddenly. It gives warning signs. First, the moisture inside the palms of the hands, then shallowness of breath and an elevated pulse. Everything in the immediate surroundings becomes a potential irritant: people who laugh too loudly, a whiff of a stale cinnamon bun, fast-moving cars, the hypnotizing flickering of the ceiling fan. Debilitating nausea and an upset stomach are laughingly predictable. But the final and most potent is a feeling of confinement and the inability to escape. The strong fight-or-flight response pumps gallons of adrenaline and cortisol into the bloodstream without any means of release. The ceiling presses down, the doorway narrows and locks, the walls collapse and press in, leaving no way out. Conversely, if an open space overpowers with its vastness, or a towering height threatens with a sudden expulsion into a bottomless chasm, the walls expand, and the floor retracts, denying any shelter or anchor.

Claudia was already back in her room, getting free of her suitcase and hand luggage. She looked around, confused, not remembering where to put each, and couldn't decide whether or not to unpack for the third time. She shoved everything aimlessly across the floor and let all items fall wherever they wished. She took off her wet jacket and hurled it against the wall. Exhausted and powerless, she threw herself on the bed, to no relief. The wet clothes rubbed harshly against her skin. Irritated, she sat up and began stripping haphazardly, partially pulling off her T-shirt, one sock, then her trousers, in search of some release. She felt cold and hot simultaneously. She thought she saw steam seeping from her pores, but the chills convinced her otherwise. She lay down in a corner of the room, away from the windows, clutching her knees. The shivering, strangely, always alleviated the tension. She had learned to let her body take the lead in this bizarre ritual. She kept breathing, in with her nose and out with her mouth, loudly, consciously, purposefully. She knew from experience that the wave in which she was drowning would soon ebb.

In another half hour, Claudia took a hot shower and tried to get a grip on her situation. She wasn't able to do much, but she could at least stay warm and think about her next steps. She went to the library to retrieve a few books to while away the afternoon, and as she browsed, she came across the diary she had stumbled upon earlier. Along with a couple of art albums, she took it up to her room.

July 8, 1965

People ask me what it's like to be married to a composer and, of course, I tell them what they want to hear. How wonderful it is to live in a home filled with music. How inspiring it is to be near someone of Herbert's stature. How exciting to attend his premieres, lectures, recitals, and banquets.

He is the most brilliant man I have ever known. A voracious reader, he understands world history and philosophy, speaks German and French fluently, knows art, both classical and modern. But most importantly, his music touches my soul and has the respect and admiration of his colleagues. I do the best I can to adapt to his greatness, even though it is not an easy task, but I see it as my calling. It requires a unique kind of woman, and I fully accept this challenge.

But people ask me what it's like, and I wish I could tell them I spent last Christmas alone. Yes, Herbert was at home, and we had our Christmas Eve dinner together, but as soon as the dessert was over, he disappeared into his study. After sitting for some time in silence, I decided to play a record of Christmas music, and that's when he scolded me for disrupting his concentration. The noise bothered him. Usually, I have to monitor for any kind of music coming from the radio or the television set. I only tune to the news and quickly turn it off afterward, lest a music program comes on unexpectedly and upsets him. I thought he would make an exception for the holiday.

I try to show interest in his work and read various

books to understand his world a little better, but I am afraid I will never connect with him on that inaccessible intellectual and artistic level on which he dwells. Even if I knew as much as he did, I don't think he could ever see me in the role of confidant or partner. On those occasions when we entertain his colleagues from the school or the Composer League, whenever I voice my opinion during a discussion, he waits for me to finish and then abruptly changes the subject. He doesn't show interest in what I like or in my activities outside of the home. As long as I maintain an environment conducive to his work, he is satisfied. He sees me strictly as his wife, a homemaker. I don't mind it, because I do enjoy that role, yet I suspect our union could be much deeper.

I did not marry Herbert. I married Herbert and his Art; or, I should say, I married his Art and Herbert. Everything in our lives is subject to this central principle: where we live, where he works, where we travel, who our friends are, when we vacation, how we spend our leisure time (if there is such a thing for him). Because of the new opera, our annual vacation to Watershed will have to be postponed. Either that, or I will go alone, and I have almost made up my mind to do so. There will certainly be no trips to Europe this year, nor even Paris, a trip he has promised me for several years.

Although he doesn't keep very long hours at the school, he teaches some of his students in our apartment. And when they have gone, he remains in his study alone. Even when we are together, we are never truly together, not in the way I see other couples—looking into each other's eyes or walking through the park in a comfortable silence. Emotionally and mentally, Herbert is always someplace else. He stares with a blank stare and doesn't listen when I speak to him. Very few things matter to him, and most everything outside of art annoys him. He is not likely to waste time on exchanging a few pleasant words with anyone outside of his music circles, or even with his friends, if their topic of conversation is too trivial for him. He is simply a fanatic, and a rude and selfish man.

People say an artist sacrifices everything for his art and his muse, and how right they are! Herbert sacrifices those closest to him. Both Rita and I are in his service and at his music's every beck and call. How apt the opera he is composing tells the story of Iphigenia who was to be sacrificed by her father, Agamemnon, to appease the goddess Artemis. Curiously, Iphigenia was willing to sacrifice herself to atone for her father's wrongs. Is Artemis the music? Is Agamemnon the composer? And Iphigenia—the composer's life, or, dare I say, the composer's wife?

14

That evening, Claudia felt uneasy about keeping the diary upstairs. She was mainly concerned Ms. Bertha might notice it missing or spot it sitting in Claudia's bedroom. Was it Ms. Bertha's writing? It was an old notebook, and clearly no new entries were being added, so perhaps she wouldn't realize it was gone, but still, what would Claudia say if the journal was found in her possession? She didn't want to hurt the woman's feelings. And of course, she couldn't ask her about its origins directly. The best thing to do would be to return it to its place in the library and maybe sneak down to read it again at an opportune time, if at all.

She crept downstairs, hoping the others were occupied elsewhere. As she approached the library, the sounds of a recording of a Bruckner symphony became more pronounced. In the leather armchair facing the piano, with his back to the door, sat Gabriel. He didn't see her. Stepping into the room, Claudia hid the diary between her elbow and torso, and she walked confidently toward the bookcase. She swiftly pushed the diary into its original spot and made her way back around to the sitting area.

"I didn't take you for a Bruckner kind of guy," she said. He turned to face her, his tilted head propped on his hand, his elbow on the armrest.

"What kind of guy did you take me for?" he asked.

"I don't know. Mahler or Brahms." She stood casually in front of him, pleased with her seamless maneuver.

"I don't care much for Mahler, and I think Brahms can be too proper and literal," he said. "Look, I know you didn't expect to find me here." He smiled, looking up at her.

"I didn't say that." She sounded more adamant than she needed to be.

"You didn't have to." He looked away, but a shadow of his smile remained, as he followed the symphony with the miniature score opened to the correct page.

"Don't tell me you can also read the score!"

"I dabble a little." He flipped through the pages.

"I'm sorry, but I just didn't picture you . . ." Claudia stumbled. "You are not a part of the program, are you?"

"No, I'm a complete outsider. Ms. Bertha allows me to visit the library when I have nothing better to do. You didn't think a working man could read and write?" he teased.

"It's not that. I suppose I've been too focused on my own world lately to notice other people. You'll have to tell me who's your favorite composer." She sat in the armchair next to his in a penitent gesture.

"Come on, you of all people should know better than to ask a cliché question like that. There is no one single person. Not even one single historical period or style." Without oars or tools to occupy his hands, he gesticulated easily. He seemed like a different man. "I suppose what draws me in is the truth, the honesty of the composer."

Claudia listened with interest.

"Would I be drawn to your music?" he asked.

"I'm not sure. Truth and honesty are difficult to define in music." She stared into the space in front of her.

"And in life?" he asked.

"In life, it's easier, though probably more painful." She sighed. "Tell me about those truthful and honest composers." She rested her head on the back of her armchair.

"Let's see, you are putting me on the spot. I haven't worked out a thesis or anything like that." He fidgeted with the score. "I think certain composers are pretentious and others are more in touch with authentic human emotions. Some composers are able to make that switch in their lifetime. Early Mozart is pearls and powder, but late Mozart is life and death. I see the same in Beethoven. Fauré's Requiem will always spell eternity for me, and not necessarily because of its religious subject. I can't stand Verdi or Grieg or Tchaikovsky, though

I like to study their scores."

"How did you become interested in music?" Claudia asked, all ears. She couldn't help shaking her head in disbelief.

"I'm not sure. I suppose it just happened on its own. Once I learned music notation, a whole new world opened up to me. But I'm probably making a fool of myself sharing my opinions so freely with you." His ears reddened a little.

"No, not at all. You have a fresh point of view," she reassured him.

"You mean non-academic."

"Yes, you could say that. But it's no less valid."

"What are you working on right now?" he asked, changing the subject.

"A cello sonata. Cello is one of my most favorite instruments," she replied. It felt good not to have to lie anymore.

"And this sonata, is it your favorite composition?"

Claudia paused. This was a strange question.

"It has been obstinate and slow in shaping up, but it's getting there," she answered carefully.

"Why is it obstinate?" He crossed his legs and tilted his head. "I don't mean to pry—I'm just curious about your process."

"I'm in the middle of what you could call a dry spell, or writer's block. That's all." She waved her hand dismissively.

"I have a hard time believing that." He smiled

again, tapping the score booklet against the armrest.

"What do you mean?" She hadn't expected him to be this familiar.

"A dry spell is for someone who doesn't have anything to say, someone who lacks in new experiences or imagination," Gabriel said.

"Well, I do have imagination and plenty of experiences, but I find myself at a crossroads right now, and honestly, I don't feel very motivated to compose," she replied with a touch of impatience.

"What's made you lose your motivation?" he probed further.

She scoffed. "Is this the moment in the conversation when you give me a laminated quote from a self-help book?" She held an imaginary rectangle with her fingers, looking him square in the eyes. "'Visualize your potential' and all that nonsense?"

"I wouldn't presume." He exhaled and looked away.

She regretted her rudeness. "I'm sorry. It's complicated," Claudia relented, leaning back into her armchair.

"Something above my pay grade?" he asked.

Absentmindedly, she let her arms dangle over the sides of her chair.

"No, it's just that . . . I don't think I have the strength to continue writing. I'm afraid I've lost faith in music. In order to compose, you have to have something to say, something to share, and I just feel . . . numb." There it was. She had said it out loud and, strangely, it brought a release.

"For someone who feels numb, you certainly put on quite a show today. Have you thought about composing music about that?"

"No. That seems too trivial to me. I think music should speak to higher ideals, transcending experiences. It should strive for the eternal, the objective." She looked up at the light fixture. "It should be completely removed from the gutter."

"I see. So you are an idealist?" he asked.

"Yes. I suppose I am." She nodded slowly.

"Why did you decide to become a composer?"

Claudia sighed and scratched her forehead. "I was looking for the meaning of life, the unifying principle." She tilted her head rhythmically from side to side, going down the list in a satirical way. "The music of the spheres, the philosophy of harmony, all that stuff, whatever people want to call it."

"And instead you found . . . ?"

Claudia drummed her fingers on the armrest. "And instead I found an environment tainted with flawed humanity."

"Not a good predicament for an idealist to find herself in."

"Not exactly."

"But what if you were wrong?" he asked.

"In what way?" She looked at him again.

"It seems to me that you put music on a

pedestal." He leaned toward her and set the miniature score aside. His hands were free to gesticulate again. "Something unattainable, something to be worshiped. But what if you let the music off the pedestal, let it become more common, more human, less divine?"

She snorted. "That's what pop music is for."

"No, I don't think it's a matter of genre or style. I'm talking about seeing the music not as a goal or a destiny, an end result, but a pathway, the means to an end, a tool in the process of creating something else." He paused to let her weigh this idea.

"Then music would have to be subservient to something else. Something greater than itself. And what could that be?" Claudia asked.

"Spoken like a true idealist. Let the music express your true humanity. Allow the music to express your true self as it is right now, not as you imagine it should be at some ideal time in the future." His gray eyes were intently focused on her.

"Then I would need a convoluted four-movement symphony to describe this whole mess." She burst into laughter.

"Yes, it's too bad you have to write this proper academic cello sonata instead." He grinned, looking away.

"I see what you're saying, but composing a symphony is a monumental undertaking. It really does require an inspired mindset and, shall we say, a divine appointment." She shook her head. "I just don't see myself as the right person for the job—even though, ironically, I recently was asked to do just that. Twice, come to think of it." She scoffed. "That task is way above my pay grade, and the timing is less than ideal."

"It's just a friendly theoretical exercise," Gabriel said. "I've spent more time with larger musical forms, so I might be biased toward the symphony."

"Well then, why not go full-scale and compose an opera or a ballet?" she challenged him.

"You want a non-academic opinion?" he asked.

"Of course," she replied, sweeping her hand toward him, opening the floor for the presentation of his argument.

He straightened and perched on the edge of his armchair.

"I think music in the opera is like wallpaper. It's there, but we don't see it. We feel it in the periphery, but the meaning is found in the libretto. Music is there to support it and to connect the plot points. The same in a ballet, where the dance conveys the meaning. But in the case of a symphony, the composer is naked before the audience, with nothing to divert its attention. Music is the only language, the only way to express a composer's intent. In my opinion, it's the highest form and the most challenging for a composer."

Gabriel's words resonated with Claudia. He didn't have the technical vocabulary of a musicologist, but his instincts were well grounded, and he supported them with specific musical examples. She was happy to get away from the usual scholarly lingo and didn't feel pressured to impress him with her credentials or to belittle his lack of institutional training. They talked for a long time about music and life. Not in a personal or a prodding way, but in general terms, in imaginary scenarios and possibilities. The sudden hiss of the needle gliding across the runout groove of the record reminded them that time could not stand still forever.

15

Following a peaceful night, Claudia woke up with a fresh perspective. She decided she would remain on the island. Yes, certain interactions had made her uncomfortable, but she was going to give the program one more chance. Perhaps she had overreacted. Her perennial struggle with anxiety certainly didn't help her judgment. And besides, these people were artists, creatives, notoriously the most challenging segment of society with which to get along. What was important was that here she had a quiet place to work, free food, a well-stocked library, a majestic forest, and a breathtaking river to soothe her senses. She was lucky to get a break from the university—a luxury many of her colleagues could only dream about.

She would make up for yesterday by spending this day productively. Right after breakfast, she set out for a brisk walk on a new, unfamiliar path lined with flowering grasses. Ignorantly, Claudia reached out to gather a bouquet, and dozens of tiny pricks pierced the top of her hand. But still, she kept grasping clusters of the buckhorn and the stinging nettles.

The forest surprised her with ever new woodlots of tree species: walnuts, pines, spruces, and firs. She wished she knew more about their habitats but for now, she could only distinguish their general shapes and scents. The multiple olfactory layers present in the woodland intrigued her. The leaves growing on the trees smelled different from those that had fallen on the ground. The evergreens emitted saps in all fragrances, and their barks, cones, and needles had distinct smells of their own. And then there was the soil, the roots, the sand, moss, mushrooms, endless varieties of shrubs. The presence of water altered all of the scents, and so did changes in temperature. Claudia thought about the harmonious coexistence and fluid relationships between all of these elements and discovered in it a system not unlike music.

She returned to her room refreshed. She pulled her manuscript sheets from her portfolio and inspected the damage from yesterday's tantrum. A couple of pages had suffered damp corners, but most others were still intact. She lined up her graph paper sketches in a row above the music, organized her pencils, and then set to work. The early structural designs of the sonata proved very effective, and now, with greater ease and efficiency, Claudia could flesh out her original musical ideas.

She found the opening of the sonata exceptionally well articulated and set out to transfer it from the sketch sheet to the more intermediate stage. She inscribed "Cello Sonata" at the top of the page and began to print her own name in the right upper corner, as has been the custom of composers for centuries. "Claudia . . ." She paused to think what the gesture represented. She signed her name to identify herself as the composer of the work, to identify herself *with* the work, to tell the world this music represented her. And then, suddenly, she realized this piece of music did not represent her at all. Not her true self. Her imaginary pretentious academic self, yes, but not the core of her authentic being.

She called herself an idealist, yet here she was, conforming to a particular institutional stereotype of what art music should be. She wrote in a style widely accepted in academic circles, one signaling familiarity with avant-garde and modernism, and yet one that did not bring anything groundbreaking or new. It merely copied the same gestures and conventions heard in recital halls for the last fifty years.

Had Gabriel been right to speak about truth in music? Was there even such a thing? What if she was unencumbered and free to write whatever she felt like, without any imposed limits of style, form, instrumentation? This music would unfold freely from her mind and flow onto the page without internal judgment or fear of rejection. She closed her eyes, imagining that music, those sounds, allowing them to fill her mind with colorful morphing shapes, flavors, scents. The warmth she sensed behind her closed eyelids began to flow downward through her face and neck, into her chest and her belly, filling her with a soothing sensation. It expanded into her upper arms and wrists, down into her fingers, and out onto the page.

She jolted from the desk, dragging the metal legs of the chair across the wooden floor. The experience frightened her, not because it was unpleasant but because it was unknown to her. She began to pace, brainstorming rapidly.

What if she did write the symphony? Not the whole symphony, of course. The task would be too monumental. But maybe just one movement or the opening section. She could dip her toes in the water and see if the idea had any merit. There was no harm in trying, and she could quit at any time. No one needed to know about her experiment. And yes, it would be "an experiment." What a wonderful noncommittal word! Her plan began to solidify. She would continue with the cello sonata and submit it as part of her thesis, but at the same time, independently, she would prepare early sketches of a symphony, in secret.

She returned to her seat. She promised herself that later she would give the symphony more thought and consider all the pros and cons. It sounded reasonable, but she needed to assess the scope of the project. Besides, she had already wasted several days, and only five weeks of her residency now remained. That was hardly enough time for a gigantic endeavor like a symphony. Regardless of what she would ultimately decide, already she felt slightly better about herself and was glad to have not only early versions of the sonata but entire passages committed to music notation. She would try to do her best with the time she had left.

16

August 4, 1965

How does a woman know? She does not. Not at first and not for certain. She only senses that something is not right. She suspects. She notices. She connects the dots, and she infers. It is not an educated guess but a nudge of instinct. That's how I knew without knowing.

And now I blame myself for not knowing sooner. I was the first to welcome Rita into our home. I was pleased Herbert would have such a talented and knowledgeable assistant. As soon as she joined him, he became more energetic and enthusiastic about his work on the opera. He told me many times the compositional process became faster, more streamlined, simpler, now that she was helping. I was always there in the apartment with them when they worked together in Herbert's study, just across the hall, with the doors wide open. All I ever heard from them was their secret composer shorthand I have learned to ignore. "Doublings here?" "Strings an octave lower." "This texture is too thick." "Should these measures line up?" "Moderato or Poco Allegro?"

I have wondered about her. Why does a woman in her late twenties spend so much time with an older married man? She lived for a couple of years in Paris among the artists, so maybe she is more liberated than the rest of us. I understand wanting a career, but music is no field for a respectable woman. I see all these chorus girls and dancers. Endless evening rehearsals, no home life, no stability, questionable morals, flawed reputations. That's not a life for someone like Rita. At her age, she should be looking for a husband—otherwise, in a few years, it might be too late for her. Herbert says assisting him will be advantageous for her career. I gather she aspires to be a composer one day. I hope she experiences all the aspects of this profession up close through observing him and that she changes her mind soon. It's strenuous enough for a man. I can't imagine any woman carrying that kind of burden.

She was always pleasant to me. Dressed appropriately, punctual, and professional. I must say I genuinely looked forward to her company, however fragmented it was. Sometimes she ran errands for Herbert, brought papers or books from school, maybe recordings. On occasion, she even ran a couple of errands for me. Nothing substantial, because I didn't want to detract from her time with Herbert.

One week, when she fell ill and was unable to come to the apartment, Herbert was agitated and impatient. I suggested a substitute, but he only mumbled something under his breath and sulked in his study. I don't know if he did any work that week at all. But then, when she returned, all fell back into place and the opera progressed. Sometimes, Lenny, the librettist, came to consult on the text, and the three of them would laugh and have a good time. I served them coffee and dessert and joined in the jovialities. When Lenny remarked on their unprecedented pace, I was only proud of Herbert.

I don't think Herbert was meeting her at the school. He spent as little time as possible there, saying he always preferred to work at home. So here they were together for hours on end under our roof. She didn't strike me as the "type," and I had no reason to be suspicious. For heaven's sake, anyone who has ever met Herbert knows he has never been a woman chaser, and any impropriety would be entirely inconsistent with his character and, dare I say it, his dull disposition.

But then, one day, in passing, I saw them in the hallway as she was preparing to leave. He helped her on with her coat and touched her forearm with such tenderness as I have not seen in years. I could not explain it, nor could I excuse it away. I tried to pretend it hadn't happened. But it did, and it began to chisel a cavity in my mind. I decided to wait before saying or doing anything rash, until I had something more substantial to prove that I wasn't wrong.

And then, one Sunday afternoon, when I was dusting Herbert's desk, I came across Rita's compact mirror. It had a round folding frame with a brass clasp and a picture of a lady with rouged cheeks and a yellow rose pinned in her hair. How ironic that this color signifies friendship. There are as many kinds of friendship as there are kinds of love. Some are yellow, some orange, and others border on pink and red. The mirror was smack in the middle of his desk, like a toy or a talisman, or a lucky charm. Whether she gave it to him, or whether he stole it from her purse, or she left it there by accident—it made no difference to me. It enraged me so, and I confronted Herbert that very evening. He didn't say much at all. Admitted nothing. Denied nothing. That's how I knew without knowing.

17

A loud knock interrupted Claudia's concentration.

"Yes?" Claudia answered without turning from her desk, anticipating Ms. Bertha wanting to check on her.

"Claudia, it's me."

She turned sharply toward the door, bracing herself against the chair-back. Diego stood on the other side of the partially open door, looking timidly in.

"I just wanted to say, you know, I was a jerk. I don't want you to be upset."

Claudia remained silent, but she bit her lip and her heart rate intensified.

"Look, you have to understand how we painters think," he continued, taking half a step inside. "I'm so tired of painting landscapes. Painting the human body is the ultimate. When I saw you, I just took a chance. Please believe me," he pleaded. "I've sketched hundreds of nudes before. It's not sexual. I don't even think about it. It's aesthetic. It's objective: the mass, the form, the light. It's not like I'm a pervert. I would hate for you to think about me that way. Please, Claudia, I'm sorry. I didn't mean . . ."

"That's all right. I'd forgotten all about it." She had not, of course, but she could let it go in exchange for being left alone.

His shoulders slackened. "Would you be willing, in a gesture of reconciliation,"—he stretched his arms toward her—"to pose for me, for a portrait? I mean, fully clothed and all, downstairs in the studio. I would like to draw your portrait as a gift. For you."

She smiled guardedly, looking down at her hands. "I don't know. I'm in the middle of something. It's very kind of you."

"Oh, come on! You've been sitting here all day. When was the last time you took a break?" He was getting more relaxed, ready to joke with her again.

She hesitated, but he was right. She did feel stiff and drained. "I suppose I could sit for a little while. If it's not going to last several hours."

"No, no, just a quick pencil sketch, nothing elaborate."

"Okay. But only for a short time," Claudia agreed.

He clapped his hands together to seal the deal and motioned for her to join him. He led her to the art studio, where he began to rearrange the canvases scattered on the floor. From the armchair situated in the middle of the room, he removed a couple of art albums and a sweater.

"Why don't you make yourself comfortable right here?" He motioned for her to sit down.

"I didn't even comb my hair." She patted her head and scratched her eyebrow.

"Oh, no need. Just as you are is perfect, *Alice Guérin*."

She sat on the edge of the armchair and started combing her fingers through her long red locks.

"That's perfect." He came near her, motioning with his hands as if to assist her, but he kept his distance and didn't touch her.

"That's great. Maybe just pull your hair forward on your shoulder. And sit farther in, lean into the armchair. Great. Perfect. Stay just like this."

He walked in silence from left to right, examining her from all angles. Self-conscious, Claudia followed him with her head.

"No, no." He grasped the air. "Don't move. Look over there."

She obeyed.

"This will be the perfect spot, I think." And with a swift push of the easel, he placed himself in front of a sheet of cream-colored paper backed with cardboard for stability. Dozens of graphite pencils stood in a glass jar on the side table. They clanked inside the container like hard candy in a cookie jar when he shuffled through them until he found the right one. He began to draw with erratic, broad gestures, glancing at her every few seconds.

"You know what's the most important thing in

a painting?" he asked without stopping.

Claudia moved the pupils of her eyes toward him, without breaking the pose.

"The light. The balance between the light and darkness. The contrast. Too much light and you have a washed-out ghost, but too much darkness and you end up with a dark blob of nothingness. My painting didn't take off until I understood this principle. It's not even about the hue or the warmth or coolness, but about the light against the dark." He continued to sketch with his right hand, and with his left, he steadied his cardboard rig. "I once saw a painting at the Frick Collection in New York. *The Harbor of Dieppe* by Turner. I have studied the paintings of so many masters; I have no idea how I never knew about this one. The most unreal realistic painting of sunlight. I think he used only two colors to paint it: chrome yellow and cobalt blue, with some white to soften them. No trace of red or green. You have to wonder if he had achromatopsia."

Claudia wasn't particularly interested in this soliloquy.

"Tell me, Diego," she interrupted, "have you been painting very long?"

"Since I was about ten years old."

"So you started as a child? You were a natural." She might as well treat this conversation as a personal research.

"A natural?" he scoffed. "There is nothing

natural about art. You know what's natural? Sleep is natural. Eating, riding a bus, shopping for socks. There is nothing natural about art."

"But the instinct to create is," she persisted without moving.

"The instinct to create art is, but creating art is not. It's a paradox. The cruelest of paradoxes—for an artist, anyway. You want to paint a sunrise, but you end up producing a yellow circle on a blue background. The struggle to get somewhere near that sunrise is more unnatural than anything I have ever known, especially after you fail a hundred times."

"But your paintings, from what I have seen here, are beautiful." She meant what she said.

"Oh, please, with all respect to your specialized training and all, you are not qualified to judge. Besides, I don't think it's even about beauty." His brashness had returned. He didn't seem cognizant of it.

"Then what? Truth?" Claudia was not offended.

"Truth? You can't be serious. If you want the truth, you can snap a photo, but even then, you'll end up only somewhere in the neighborhood of the truth. I want to be as far away from the truth as possible." He leaned out from behind his easel, squinting at her. He did not see her as a person, but as an object to be measured. "With my art, I want to create an alternative reality, a parallel universe that will swallow me up when I work and swallow up the viewer when the painting is displayed. This desire and this whole artistic struggle BS are unnatural. They mess with your mind. Sometimes, honest to goodness, I wish I could just work at a convenience store and have a normal life."

"Yes, I have wanted that for myself, too," Claudia said.

"Then let's go into business together!" he exclaimed excitedly.

"What would we sell?" She looked at him.

"What else? Aspirin, lottery tickets, and hot dogs," he said.

They laughed together.

"What's so funny?" asked Stephanie.

She stood at the entrance to the studio, dressed in a tight-fitting ruffled pink dress. Smiling, she turned from Claudia to Diego, then back to Claudia, waiting for an answer. Someone ought to explain to the girl how to tone down the overdressing, but it wasn't going to be Claudia who wore her gray yoga pants and stretched-out brown sweater.

"We are going into business together. We are opening a convenience store," Diego said triumphantly.

Stephanie laughed and stepped inside.

"Come on, Stephy, sit by Claudia," said Diego, gesturing for her to join them. "I'll draw you in. Here, sit on the armrest and lean against Claudia. I think you'll fit in the frame. Yes, that's good."

Stephanie sat on the right armrest, a foot or so above Claudia, and leaned in, putting her left arm around her. Her sizable breast pressed softly into Claudia's bony shoulder. She rested her head on Claudia's and smiled a big toothy smile. Though Claudia felt a bit smothered, she kept her pose. Stephanie's fragrance, a subtle yet unmistakable lily of the valley, permeated the air. Her feminine aura was compelling, encroaching.

"You two look like sisters," Diego remarked. "Stephy told me you might be writing a symphony; is that true?" he asked.

"Well, I don't know if . . . . I'm still working on my cello sonata." Claudia took a deep breath and tensed the muscles of her neck. "But I did some very preliminary sketches of a symphony. It's nothing serious, more like an experiment."

"Oh, that's great, Claudia!" Diego enthused. "I knew you two would hit it off. Stephanie, could you move your left hand here?" He motioned from behind the easel. "Yes, move it down to Claudia's waist. That's better."

Claudia readjusted her position, shuffling her feet. Her lower back was stiff, and she didn't appreciate this invasion of her personal space. She wanted to ask how much longer she would have to sit in this uncomfortable pose, but before she could open her mouth, Diego continued:

"I knew you would understand Stephy. I love

her very much, but as a painter, I can't really help her. I haven't understood it until now. And now that you're here, it makes perfect sense." He was still engrossed in his sketch. "She tried to explain this to me before, but I just wouldn't listen. I was too stubborn to see it. But now, with you, it was meant to be. I'm really happy for you two."

Claudia was baffled. Was this some kind of artsy New Age talk? Or was he indulging Stephanie in a delusion? Was he handling her, pacifying her? Or was he sending Claudia an encoded message she was too ignorant to comprehend? She looked at him but could detect no attempt at nonverbal communication. He kept glancing at them in adoration and swept his pencil across the page. Claudia counted the seconds till she could excuse herself from this awkward situation.

"There," said Diego. "I'll work some more on the shading, but you are free to go. Thank you so much, Claudia. I'll give you the drawing later."

Claudia smiled politely and left as quickly as she was able. Pain had entered her neck, and her right foot was a touch numb. She walked awkwardly up the stairs and paused at the landing. Downstairs in the office, Victor, in a muffled voice, spoke to someone on the phone. She lingered for a few seconds in order to listen to the conversation.

". . . So when are you going to get here? I miss you."

". . ."

"Okay. Did you have a good trip?"

". . ."

"I know. I remember. That doesn't surprise me at all." He laughed.

". . ."

"Not well. I wrote a strong opening, but right now everything is turning into mush—sentimental adolescent mush. I think I'll have to stir things up a bit. Either this or rewrite it."

". . ."

"You could say that again. I'll let you know. Well, hurry up! Kisses."

Claudia tiptoed all the way into her room, quietly closing the door behind her.

18

September 5, 1965

I had to ask Herbert to dismiss Rita, but he kept telling me how talented and unique she is and that I am clipping her wings. Is it me who is doing the clipping, or is it she herself, or even Herbert? I bet there are a dozen just like her waiting to fill her spot. If the little harlot really wants to be a composer, she can weasel herself in some other way. Another composer might need an assistant, but how is Herbert going to recommend her to anyone now? That is not my concern. I simply want her gone from my home! I don't care if she has to look for work at a secretarial agency.

Herbert assures me nothing happened—nothing physical, that is. That they had a unique connection only and were musical colleagues, and that, yes, she was devoted to him and adored his music! (Who doesn't?) He said she was a perfect assistant, who knew exactly how to orchestrate his sketches, and that most of the time she practically read his mind. That he didn't have to train her or correct her mistakes. That she was familiar with his composition style, instinctively adding her own touches he found both groundbreaking and inspiring.

I could not abide listening to these technical accolades. I almost wish something physical did happen! At least then I would have something concrete to rage against, but this way, I am upset about the ambiguity of the situation. If nothing happened, then who was she to him exactly? A muse? An inspiration? That would be worse than a mistress. For a composer it might be more meaningful than some momentary fleshly indulgence. I can't stand the idea that another woman, apart from me, might approach or inhabit that sacred space fueling his creative desires.

Or was she a type of a daughter to him? And if so, would it be so much nobler? Wouldn't it mock my inability to have children? I certainly never felt motherly toward her, and she never gave the impression of needing to be mothered—or fathered, for that matter. Herbert used the word "mentor" frequently, but it didn't sit well with me. Let a man mentor another man, and let women be mentored by women. It prevents a lot of misunderstandings and keeps people from making up stories.

Poor Herbert. It could be a symptom of a mid-life crisis, a realization of the passing of time and a fascination with youth. She is still so young and with so much to look forward to. I wish I could be her age again. God, how it hurts that I will never be young again and that Herbert will never look at me the way he looked at her. The puzzling thing is that she is not particularly pretty. She isn't dreadful, but she does seem rather plain and ordinary to me. All the more mystery why Herbert was so taken with her.

I made a big scene, demanding he get rid of her at once. I told him he could find a substitute and continue his work, or he could move to his office at the school permanently. I stood my ground, but I swear the pained expression on his face nearly broke my heart. It hurt me to say these things, for the first time in our marriage, but I needed to say them in order to save it. Forgive me, Herbert, but I love you, and I hope that, in time, you will see this was the best course of action.

He let her go. All it took was a quick phone call. I didn't hear their conversation, because for the first time in a long time, he closed the door to his study. After he was done, he left the apartment for a few hours. I don't know where he went or what he did. I was afraid to ask. When he returned, he didn't eat supper that night. A week passed before he resumed working on his opera, but his enthusiasm for it was gone.

19

Claudia was slowly constructing a new work routine for herself. An early morning walk, followed by a light breakfast, a focused composing session with a quick break for lunch, then another segment of music writing or some research in the library. Dinner with Ms. Bertha or on her own, and more reading in the evening—or occasionally a chat with the other residents. The cello sonata was taking shape, and Claudia was pleased with the results. She was confident she would finish in time to tie the work into her thesis and submit everything before the deadline.

This day was a pleasant one. Claudia felt unrushed, in control. Productivity always gave her a sense of balance and well-being. She did a load of laundry and ironed her clothes. She noticed Ms. Bertha had left a few towels in the dryer and folded them for her. She even took pity on a fainting succulent on the windowsill and revived it with a few drops of water.

For her lunchtime meal, she reheated some chicken soup on the stove and took it to the dining room for a change of scenery. She ate in silence, admiring the display of silver spoons in one of the curio cabinets near the honey-colored fringed drapery.

"Good afternoon, Claudia!" Richard's voice behind her interrupted her meandering thoughts.

"Hello, Richard." She turned to face him, but he was already making his way to the other side of the table, heading for the chair across from her.

How should she behave? A cold shoulder, a professional detachment, indifference? She couldn't decide on her facial expression but eventually settled on a light smile. He, in turn, gave the impression of someone who wanted to show off the results of his recent dental cleaning.

"So good to see you again!" he proclaimed.

She was glad he had taken the seat across the table, or else he might reach out and hug her, heaven forbid.

"Claudia, I'll get straight to the point. I need to apologize for our previous conversation. I acted a little prematurely in asking you to write the symphony. I was under a lot of stress, and I suppose I didn't think it through as thoroughly as I should have." He rested one of his elbows on the polished table, drumming his fingers on the surface. Claudia stopped her silver spoon mid-air.

"And I should tell you that I acted independently of Adrienne. She had nothing to do with it. It was solely my idea." His smile disappeared, and he looked down to gather his thoughts before continuing. "When I told her, she was very upset with me. Very upset." He shook his head. "I now understand it was inappropriate and I hope you will be so kind as to forget about the whole incident. Your refusal was entirely justified, and I am glad you decided against it." He stared straight at Claudia, and his habitual overpowering smile returned.

"Thank you, Richard," Claudia began, slowly. "I don't think much more needs to be said on the topic. I had nearly forgotten about it." She stirred the soup in the ceramic bowl, but she wasn't about to fill her mouth with food in case the conversation was to continue.

Richard hesitated. He smoothed the tabletop with his palm. "And I think you were right when you first mentioned that you might not be the ideal person for this project as far as the style is concerned."

Claudia waited for him to finish the thought.

"You see, the judges in the competition usually look for a certain finesse and sophistication, a certain edge in the sonic approach, something that perhaps you don't possess in your musical language." He spoke softly but deliberately.

Insolent bastard! She rested the spoon in the bowl and took her hands off the table, looking him square in the eyes. She tightened her jaw.

"And please, don't take this as a criticism at all," he continued. "This is simply a matter of personal taste and stylistic preference, nothing more."

She wanted to walk away, but he went on talking, all the while examining his manicured fingers, adorned with a bulky class ring and a sizable, diamond-encrusted wedding band.

"I think, in your own interests, you should focus on your cello sonata, not only because this was the original project you chose for this residency, but also because I can now see clearly that you are better suited for it."

"Well, I just . . ." she stammered. She sensed the blood pulsating in her temples. She was no match for Richard's intimidating manner.

"Larger forms," he interrupted, "such as the symphony, as you know, require a greater sense of commitment and personal sacrifice. And, let's be honest, not everyone possesses these qualities." He smirked. "For the sake of your career and the stage of life in which you find yourself, with the writing of your thesis and the responsibilities of teaching, the cello sonata is a very safe choice for you, very safe indeed."

"My writing is going very well right now." She didn't feel as though being rude in return would be a wise move, but she ended up sounding weak and feeble.

"Do you have anyone in mind to premiere it?" he asked.

"I'm not sure yet." She wanted to give her voice a little more impetus and she cleared her throat. "I think I will ask my colleague at the university, the head of the strings department."

"Oh, yes, that will be a suitable venue for your work. I believe we must be more in tune with the needs of the local community and make more effort to serve the underprivileged. I know this is something Adrienne will want to incorporate into her outreach. She hasn't had much time thus far because of her international career."

He mocked Claudia, and she was just sitting there, taking it, belittled and powerless, with her legs pulled tightly under her chair. She rested her arms on the table again, as if to brace herself.

"Well, I'm not certain I would look at it this way. The university—"

"Another thing to consider, perhaps," he interrupted her, "is the timing. You see, the music field is so very unique." He squinted. "As you know, it is imperative that young children begin rigorous training as soon as possible to increase their chances of full artistic development and success." He waved his index finger. "Adrienne, of course, started very early, and she succeeded very early as well—very early." He closed his eyes and raised his eyebrows. "I think those who have not shown extraordinary achievements by the age of, say, fifteen, have little chance of success later on, wouldn't you agree?"

Claudia was livid. Her lungs shook, sending shivers through her entire torso. She wasn't going to tolerate this arrogant asshole anymore.

"I'm not sure I can agree—" She raised her voice, but only ever so slightly.

"I see it over and over again." He didn't seem to hear her. "They waste their time. People who fill our institutions, who merely provide a background for the few stars, the truly gifted." His distant gaze returned to her. "But, I'm sorry, I've somehow digressed." He chuckled. "I'm sure you will do very well with your cello sonata."

He reached his hand across the table but was too far for a handshake or a pat on the shoulder. Instead, he tapped the surface in front of Claudia's soup bowl.

"I have much faith in you, and I wish you all the best. All the best. I hope you get to explore the pine forest. It's a sight to behold."

He stood and left as quickly as he had come. Claudia remained seated, unable to eat. She was devastated, trampled, bulldozed.

20

There was absolutely no chance Claudia could compose any music that afternoon. She needed to leave the villa, to go somewhere, anywhere, anywhere else. She put on a jacket and took a scarf just in case she were to stay out late into the evening and ran out of the house with no specific plan but to disappear into the woods, to walk off her anger. She kept marching until the villa was out of sight, behind a hill.

She ran down into a ravine. The light was more diffused down here, and small particles of dust floated in the long narrow sunbeams streaking through the trees. Stubby barren branches stuck out in all directions from the lower sections of the tall pines, but overhead, the crowns were lush and thick with fragrant needles. They protected Claudia from all sides, tucking her into a secret hiding place.

She grasped one of the tree trunks with both hands. The gray-brown bark was rough, dry, and cracked like parched soil. She pressed her cheek against it. The wood smelled like tranquility, but Claudia's mind was still racing. Her breathing intensified, and she couldn't quiet her thoughts.

She tried, in every possible way known to her, to relax, but she was on the cusp of an explosion. She shook the trunk with all her strength and screamed with all the savageness her throat allowed. The sound didn't echo but was immediately muffled, swallowed by the cliffs on either side of her and the thick moss layer beneath. She yelled and shook the tree again and again, until her rage began to abate. There was no response from the forest or from anyone, only the quiet rustling of the leaves and the soft creaking of branches. The steadfastness of nature pacified her. It was immovably present. It witnessed her struggles without taking sides or giving advice. It grounded her, upheld her, listened to her.

Ordinarily, in such a stressful situation, Claudia would experience a panic attack, or at least carefully balance on the very edge of one, but this time, the anger welling inside of her didn't tear her down, but instead built an energizing momentum. It surprised her and amused her. Yes, she felt belittled and offended by Richard, but at the same time, strangely, her inner spirit was rising. She was tired of feeling and acting like a victim. She would turn the tide and change her circumstances. She would show that bastard and Adrienne and all of them—the entire broken system. She would prove to them she wasn't done yet, that she would live on her own terms, would carve her own path.

Maybe because of the crisp forest air or her

restful night, Claudia's mind was exceptionally clear. She was struck with an instant and powerful insight. She decided that she, Claudia Morton, would abandon writing the cello sonata and would instead compose the symphony for no one else but herself, and that she would write it in the style that damn well pleased her alone, without giving thought to anyone's taste, aesthetic expectations, academic cynicism, or practical considerations. It would be a large-scale orchestral work in four movements. And if she had to delay her dissertation to write it, so be it.

As soon as this scenario unfolded in her mind, she felt lighter and happier. She walked farther into the thicket, touching every clump of grass and tree trunk on her way, feeling their coarseness, smoothness, waviness, roundness, softness. Every twig, leaf, and conifer suddenly fascinated her, as if she had turned a new chapter, as if she had entered a new era.

She began calculating how long it might take her to write the symphony. She knew her average speed for composing chamber music, but it was impossible merely to multiply that quantity by the number of orchestral instruments. She would have to approach it differently. It would be unlike anything she had ever created. Did she have enough manuscript paper? No, not likely. But she could use it for sketching and prepare more advanced drafts in her music notation software on her laptop. She would find a way! And the library had so many scores and recordings to help her gather ideas. She felt excited, encouraged, strengthened.

She imagined meeting Richard again and saying to him, "Thank you, Richard, for stirring these powerful emotions in me and for helping me find the courage to believe in myself, you sanctimonious, conceited, pompous bastard!" She laughed at this thought. It was cathartic.

She picked up her pace and breathed deeply of the river air. She had to be close to the shore now. Yes, the sparkling water peered through the vegetation, but Claudia didn't recognize the tall oaks surrounding her. Feeling disoriented, she decided to simply follow the shore until she came across a familiar setting. She walked along through thick ferns and white birches. The forest was always the same yet always different, depending on the time of day and the direction from which she viewed it.

A few minutes later, she noticed a familiar sight in the distance. It was Gabriel's small pier, although it looked larger from this angle. His boat was tied down, but he was nowhere near. She walked back and forth along the shore before stepping onto the pier. She stood motionless for a few moments, but then walked over toward the boat, climbed in, and sat down on the bench to rest. The water bent the light in abstract zigzags. A willow flycatcher squirmed in the tall marshy grass. She turned to the sun and closed her eyes. The afternoon was warm, serene, and ripe.

"I see you're ready for another adventure." Gabriel was approaching along the pier.

"I'm sorry, I didn't mean to . . . I just sat down for a minute." She scratched her thigh. "I hope you don't mind. I need to get back to the villa anyway." She stood up and began to clamber out of the vessel.

"No need to rush on my account." He offered his hand to assist her and she took it.

"Have you been busy? Did you get a chance to repair the boat, make the cosmetic changes?" Self-consciously, she motioned toward it, while brushing her hair from her forehead.

"Yes, it's all done; she's all new," he replied.

"It looks great. You did a great job."

"Thank you. And how have you been? Are you working hard? How's your cello sonata coming along?" He moved to the edge of the dock; he had a backpack slung over his shoulder.

"I've been very busy with the sonata, and it is going well, but I think I'm going to change direction," she said enthusiastically.

"Yes?" His eyes widened.

"I've decided—you're not going to believe it—but I've decided to compose a symphony instead." She blushed; she wasn't quite sure if she should utter these words out loud.

"That's great! Did our conversation have anything to do with it?" He patted her forearm gently. He seemed genuinely happy for her.

"Maybe. I don't know. Partially." She shrugged her shoulders and grinned.

"I'm happy I had something to do with this new development—even partially." He paused and looked at her with warmth and kindness. "I'm very happy for you, Claudia. I know you'll do great work. I imagine you'll be doubly busy right now, though."

"Quadruply busy," she answered, animated. "Well, listen, I need to get back to the villa, but I just wanted to say that I really enjoyed our conversation the other day." She toyed with the collar of her blouse. "You are an intriguing man, full of surprises," she added.

"Well, thank you, Claudia. You are no less intriguing yourself." He put his hands in the pockets of his jacket. "But I'll be gone for a few days."

A tinge of disappointment wrinkled her brow. "Maybe when you get back, we could . . ." She didn't know how to complete this sentence.

"I'm not sure when I'll be back. You shouldn't wait for me." He scratched his chin and gave her a quick, unsteady glance.

"I see," she said quietly. "I think I misunderstood. I'm sorry." Her smile tainted, she stood motionless, looking aside.

"It's not that. It's difficult to explain right now." He clung to the strap of his backpack with both hands. "I think maybe later when we have more time to talk about it."

"Yes, of course." She took a step back.

"Claudia, what's important right now is that you have a symphony to compose. You should concentrate on that. These next few weeks will be crucial for you. I wouldn't want you to waste your time on anything else." His forehead wrinkled.

"No, of course not," she whispered to herself.

Claudia felt warm and cold, happy and sad, fulfilled and disappointed. How was it possible to be entirely certain and utterly unsure all at the same time? She began heading for the villa without turning around, but every resonant part of her body could feel Gabriel dropping his backpack in the boat, untying the rope, pushing away from the pier, sloshing the water, and finally engaging the engine, whose aggressive loudness gradually diminished into a mute absence. The sound of chirping crickets, buzzing dragonflies, and jumping fish permeated the air. She hated herself for this ability to hear every speck of noise in a three-dimensional quadraphonic matrix, all parts separate and all layered together as a solid block. Her fine-tuned aural perception made everything that much more painful.

21

October 2, 1965

The name of Herbert's new assistant is John. A polite young man from the school, he is one of Herbert's recent graduates. Dressed modestly but formally, he usually wears a jacket and tie, and his shoes are always polished. I judge people by the quality of their shoes. You can tell so much about their status in society and their character. Sloppy people tend to wear sloppy shoes, but conscientious people wear clean shoes that match their outfits. I like having John around.

He has been very helpful so far, and besides assisting Herbert, he agrees to run to the dry cleaner's and even does some light shopping—something I was always hesitant to ask of Rita. John is punctual and polite and always says, "Yes, ma'am," and, "No, sir." I am glad things worked out this way, and I think Herbert will, in time, agree.

Herbert has returned to working on the opera full steam. He is just as busy and absentminded as before. But he is still adjusting to John, trying to teach him the ropes of orchestration. Maybe not so much the art of it; for that, I'm sure, John understands from his studies, but rather

Herbert's particular style of orchestration. John is indecisive, incessantly asking Herbert all kinds of technical questions: "Do you want the trombones to double in octaves here?" "Do you want to reinforce the cellos with basses there?" "How long is the crescendo here?"

Herbert is struggling to remain patient, but I can sense this is slowing him down. He has to guide the boy's hand through every measure, every line. I hope things improve with time and that they will be able to work out a more efficient relationship.

John has been with us for only the last two weeks and is still somewhat quiet and shy, but Herbert tells me not to be deceived by appearances. He said the young man has a whole other persona when he returns to his neighborhood downtown. This intrigued me immensely, but seeing how Herbert seemed to disapprove of him, I waited for John to tell me more about it himself.

It took a bit of prodding and patience, but it looks like John, to Herbert's chagrin, has abandoned many of his musical convictions and fallen into the hippie scene downtown. It would be one thing to succumb to rock and roll, but he runs with the people who get together in their apartments in the Village, or even as far as Church Street, to experiment with strange sounds. Something made with the tape recorder and electronic machines. John thinks that musical instruments, as we know them today, will be replaced by new technologies. He tells me that music scores and traditional notation are relics of the past and that listeners everywhere will have to embrace a new kind of improvisation—one that is even more progressive than what the jazz musicians are doing now. And he doesn't stop there. He and his friends are intent on reforming even the audience and will no longer allow listeners to sit in silence but ask them to walk around through their sound- and light-emitting mazes, or even to lie down on the floor. This is all very shocking, and I doubt the general public will ever be open to such radicalism. No wonder Herbert avoids this topic and John lowers his voice when he speaks about it with me. But I must admit, I find it extremely curious and fascinating and wish I could find a pretext to visit one of his happenings. If only I had someone to accompany me.

Herbert is still sulking, but I will give him credit for perseverance. He hasn't mentioned Rita at all and has thrown himself back into composing. His work is the perennial answer to all pains and disappointments of life.

22

A symphony in four movements, thirty minutes long, at least. Maybe even forty. That's seven and a half to ten minutes per movement. Claudia began calculating the time and effort required to produce the colossal composition. Her new unbridled enthusiasm encountered its first muzzle. The weight of this ambitious endeavor crushed her. How long had it taken Mozart to compose a symphony? A couple of weeks? But he had operated within a limited set of templates, clearly defined traditional structures, harmonic expectations. What about the latter composers: Bruckner, Honegger, Nielsen? They had pushed the boundaries of established forms, inventing new harmonies. How long had it taken them? Several months? A year? Claudia wished for a few megabytes of an Internet connection to perform cursory research, but even without consulting the exact timeframes, she knew she had bitten off more than she could realistically chew.

The problem of living on this side of modernism was the overwhelming freedom. To a contemporary composer, any sound combination was permissible. Any instrumental pairing, any harmony, any rhythmic and melodic pattern. The freedom was exhilarating but also paralyzing, debilitating. How would she know if she was headed in the right direction? What would guide her choices? There was no handbook for writing symphonies, no guidelines, no hotline she could call. Her advisor at the university had never even written a symphony. All he could do was refer her to a score study of works that were likely at least twenty years old. Claudia felt alone, defeated.

She pulled out her early sketches of the cello sonata and lined them in a row on the floor, next to the window. She sat cross-legged in front of them, propping up her head in her hands, taking an overview of the entire piece. It now seemed insubstantial, naïve, frail. The cello lines were just a collection of forgettable note sequences. The motives she may have found innovative before didn't seem to carry any meaning now. The piano accompaniment was dull, lifeless, academically correct and emotionally neutered.

She didn't want to continue with the sonata, but neither was she ready to begin the symphony. Her mind felt stagnant like thick maple syrup. Her thoughts were glued to the sticky immobilizing liquid. She was getting drowsy.

Putting all technical issues aside, why was she even attempting to compose a symphony to begin with? She had no chance of ever hearing it performed. The university orchestra only played the standard repertoire of Romantic composers and rarely featured modern works. If, on a rare occasion, it did so, it would be an eight-to-ten-minute short piece by a well-known composer, one whom the audience would tolerate as an appetizer to a meatier Tchaikovsky or Dvořák. The situation wasn't any better with professional orchestras. If she were to attempt the symphony, she would likely be writing it only for her own satisfaction. She could try to tie it to her dissertation and have it reviewed by the committee, but only in theoretical, academic terms.

She thought about her students, whose enthusiasm, ignorance, and naïvety kept her tied to the system she despised. She genuinely tried to nurture and guide them, to instill in them the utmost respect for the sacredness and transcendence of the art of music, while she herself secretly doubted her chosen path. She knew most of her students would eventually abandon music as a profession. She often felt guilty for prolonging the illusion. Yet, at other times, it seemed that very illusion was the only thing worth living for. She couldn't decide whether she was a hustler in a pyramid scheme, or a hospice nurse administering morphine to a dying world.

She eased onto the floor beside her bed and lay facing the brown wooden ceiling. She counted the number of planks perpendicular to the exposed trusses. She wanted to stay like that for the remainder of the day, listening to the wind and the rustling of leaves. She picked up her manuscript paper and covered herself with it as if it were a blanket. Surprisingly, it did offer some warmth. She rolled onto her side and pulled the paper over her face. Now she was in a cocoon allowing in only soft, filtered light.

The worst part about being a composer was that, as much as she was needed and appreciated as a teacher, counselor, and a lecturer, she was entirely disposable as an artist. There was no demand for her music. If she stopped writing tomorrow and never lifted her pen again, the world would go on as it had before she was even born. This dreadful realization killed any creative inkling she might have had.

She envied her friend who had opened a physical therapy practice and whose professional gratification was immediate and tangible in the form of healthy thankful patients and a healthy paycheck. Every day, his strong skillful hands thawed frozen shoulders, calmed inflamed muscles, realigned bruised hips, and straightened curved spines. His work brought concrete results he could be proud of. It had meaning, value, objective worth. Hers had none of that.

In the past few months, as the deadline for turning in her dissertation approached, Claudia had begun to doubt her station. Her chosen profession deeply discouraged her, even before she had entered it officially. Was this indeed what she was supposed to do? She had studied music most of her life. The financial commitment was sizable with a hefty student debt awaiting her at graduation. Was it too late to turn around? To start over? To do what exactly? Get another degree? Retrain? Abandon music entirely? Could she find another profession related to music? A different main course with music as a side dish? Music on the weekends? Music in the evenings? Music as a hobby? Could she turn her back on music entirely? Quit music? Abandon music? Forsake, betray, and escape music? Silence it, kill it?

Her mind raced in circles. She wished she had someone with whom to share these troubling thoughts. Someone who wouldn't judge her for feeling this wretched way, but she was utterly alone.

She pressed the paper to her face and covered her ears with it. She wasn't afraid to crumple it or to tear it. All she wanted was to escape, if only momentarily, and sleep always brought some measure of relief. She was too tired to climb up into bed, so she remained on the floor. The wind pushed against the sides of the villa, swaying her cradle back and forth, back and forth, slowly, evenly, rhythmically.

23

Claudia slept for an hour, or the whole afternoon, or three days. It made no difference. Once again, she missed Ms. Bertha's dinner time. She would try to make up for it tomorrow, maybe even help her cook. Should she offer to do that? She wasn't sure what was expected of her, yet she also knew that nothing was expected of her. She was here to compose uninterrupted, free of any chores or physical constraints. It was the premise of the entire retreat. But she wasn't working, was she? She was fumbling around, wasting time, taking the space from another artist who would have utilized the resources more wisely, would have been more focused. Guilt was the icing on this multilayered cake of self-torture.

Hungry and still groggy, she headed to the kitchen in search of food, but in her loneliness was lured by the chatting and laughter that spilled from the art studio into the hallway. She peered in at Diego and Victor slouched on the leather couch, while behind one of the easels, Stephanie was attempting to paint the scene.

"Ah, here's the culprit!" exclaimed Victor,

raising his hand in salute.

"Welcome, *Lady of Shalott*! Come, join us!" cried Diego. "You look terrible." The men laughed.

It was true. Claudia was drowning in a large sweatshirt and dragging one of her slippers, trying not to lose it on the way.

"Sit between them. I'll paint you in," said Stephanie.

"No, thank you. I'm not in the mood," said Claudia. Even if she were in the mood, it would have been pointless. Stephanie's painting was nothing but a child's doodle and splatters of brown and dark green paint.

"What's going on?" Claudia asked lazily.

"Nothing's going on; that's the whole point," said Victor. He had a beer bottle in hand, his eyes narrowed and glossy. He seemed on the verge of being drunk.

"Have you been working? How's the novel?" she asked, seating herself in a chair nearby.

"As I said, nothing's going on. It doesn't seem like you've been working either, have you?" His tone was accusatory.

"I can't find my bearings at the moment," Claudia answered, casually pulling an arts magazine off the side table and flipping through it.

"Well, there it is!" Victor slapped the leather armrest.

"Give her a break. I'm sure she's trying," Diego said. Claudia looked at them carefully. Stephanie kept pushing the paint around the canvas.

"Any new paintings, Diego?" asked Claudia without enthusiasm, mindlessly scanning the magazine.

"No, I can't paint right now," he answered. He was unshaven, his face greasy and sullen. His gray shirt was wrinkled, in need of a good washing.

"Why not?" she asked.

"My achromatopsia has gotten worse in the last few days. I'm pretty much down to grayscale." He rubbed his eyes, yawning.

"I'm very sorry to hear that. What made it worse? Can it improve?" She looked at him in concern.

"It's genetic, so it's always there in the background and is usually triggered by the environment."

"Do you mean the weather, the air?" Claudia asked.

"No, I mean this place, the villa," Diego answered, annoyed.

"It's all up to you, Claudia," Victor said, sarcastically, and he lifted the bottle, toasting her.

Claudia was puzzled but laughed it off.

"Whatever triggers your condition, Diego, I hope it can be alleviated. It must be devastating for a painter. I didn't know it was so serious." She returned the magazine to the side table. "Can you at least—I'm sorry, I don't know the mechanics of it—but can you at least draw with a black pencil for now?"

"That's all I've bloody been able to do for the last few days!" He shot up and began pacing in front of the couch. "It's so frustrating when you want to paint in full color, you know? Being here on Watershed with all this nature and time on your hands, and to be unable to draw a damn thing but black-and-white shapes. That's not what I signed up for!" He threw himself back on the couch and draped his arm across his forehead.

"Don't worry, Diego, you'll get over it. Give it time." Stephanie leaned out from behind the easel. "Victor has been writing, though," she added.

"You have?" asked Claudia with interest.

"I don't know. Yes, you could say that," Victor answered, "but I've reached a tricky point in my plot. I just don't know which way my protagonist will go and how to propel her in the right direction."

"Well, it seems to me like you give your characters too much freedom. Show them who the writer is." She laughed at her own joke. "What do you usually do in situations like this?" she asked.

"I keep throwing in more plot twists until they cave."

"Cave?" She leaned toward him.

"Well, the story has to make a dramatic turn. Otherwise, it's just a waste of time for me and the reader. Right now, I'm definitely stuck."

"I know what you mean. I can't get started on my symphony, either. It's like I hit this massive existential crisis. Can you hit writer's block before you even start?" Claudia mocked herself.

"All of you are so pathetic!" Stephanie burst out. "I'm not sure I can take it much longer. There is absolutely no inspiration in this place. No one is creating anything meaningful. I feel bad for Ms. Bertha's efforts." She squeezed herself onto the couch next to Diego, and he started rubbing her shoulders.

"That's exactly how I felt earlier," said Claudia. "I thought about Ms. Bertha and felt guilty for not composing."

"Well, at least Victor is working. Without him, this whole place would fall apart," said Diego. "Keep on writing, man, we need you. Writing crap is better than not writing at all, am I right?" He punched Victor's shoulder in a masculine display of fondness.

"I suppose. I've written some placeholders for now. I may need to rewrite the entire middle section." He was staring into the bottle, his concentration waning. "We'll see what happens after the next plot twist. But, man, I am running out of ideas here."

"And what are you up to, Stephy?" asked Diego. "I haven't heard you sing at all in the last few days. Have you taken it to the forest?" He pulled her closer to him.

"You could say that I'm also on hold." She sighed. "It's not how I imagined this retreat at all.

People always talk about Watershed as this fantastic, inspiring place where they experience something magic and surreal, but all I see here is this endless forest. Trees, more trees, and this claustrophobic house! This seclusion thing is not working for me at all." She pushed herself to the edge of the couch, shrugging off Diego's embrace. "Why don't we go to the mainland for a day trip?"

"Maybe it's the change of the seasons—you know, like the air pressure, or seasonal affective disorder," Claudia suggested, ignoring Stephanie's proposal.

"That's not till late fall and winter," said Victor. "I think it's something more immediate, something in this house."

"Like what?" asked Claudia, straightening uneasily.

"Like our internal dynamics. Like one person who breaks the chain of creativity and ruins it for the rest of us, and we fall like dominoes. There's your magic and your surrealism," Victor replied, looking at Stephanie.

"I don't believe in magic." Claudia waved him off.

"What do you believe in?" asked Diego, sighing.

"Hard work, mental focus, perseverance," she answered.

"And is it working out for you?" Victor gazed at her intently.

Claudia smiled while looking away. She stood up and yawned. "There will be no magic until I put something in my stomach. I haven't eaten all day. When your discussion on phenomenology brings a solution to getting us out of this funk, please let me know."

She exited the studio, dragging her slipper, and trying to tie her messy hair into a ponytail.

24

December 2, 1965

The last few weeks have been uneventful. Herbert, of course, is working on the opera, but I have been planning a few social occasions and the upcoming benefit gala at the school. I take immense joy in knowing that everything is organized and progressing like a well-oiled machine. I am good at anticipating things, so I am rarely surprised, whether by people or by circumstances. I live by my calendar and the desk agenda, and nothing can throw me off balance. I have scheduled and planned most of the events between now and the New Year and into February.

I sometimes wonder whether music composition is like that. Does the composer make a plan and then put the notes in the right places? Does he plan musical events? Does he make lists of elements required, leading into them? Does he follow a path he has created for himself? It could be. I have seen Herbert's preliminary sketches with time stamps and cryptic geometric markings. Still, the mystery is in where to place the individual notes, how many, how densely. I could never ask him about it.

I should start thinking about the spring and make

plans for our annual trip to Watershed. We didn't go in the summer, and if Herbert doesn't want to go this time either, I will probably have to travel alone, if for nothing else than to check on the villa. And no, I wouldn't mind a few days in nature all to myself, away from the city. I miss the pine forest and bird watching very much.

John has been of great help to Herbert, of course, just as I predicted. They may finally have found their common shorthand, because they are working in silence now. For the most part, anyway. A few days ago, Herbert had to scold John. Apparently, the young lad committed some grievous elemental mistake, one Herbert could not abide, and sent him home early in anger. I saw John as he was gathering his things; he was fuming, his face all red, and he left without a word, only a polite nod to me. I think it's good that young people learn about discipline and hard work. They can't have everything handed to them on a silver platter. John must have made an ignorant mistake, or Herbert would not have behaved as he did. I have never known him to be given to outbursts.

The next day, John returned to us, and Herbert greeted him warmly, as if nothing had happened. John had the good sense to retrieve Herbert's briefcase, which Herbert had forgotten at school the day before, and he was so happy to be reunited with his pens and notebooks. Like me, Herbert loves fountain pens and quality paper, but he has always been scatterbrained and absentminded about them. Even more so in the midst of a grand project like this opera. I feel he might be overwhelmed with everything, and who wouldn't be? How does one keep track of the endless piles of manuscript paper, revisions in several stages, more changes from the librettist, requests from the soloists, orchestrations and piano reductions, formatting of parts for rehearsals? I truly see the benefit of having a personal assistant like John to keep Herbert focused and organized.

Recently, Herbert has been spending more time with me, which leaves me equally grateful and astonished. He doesn't isolate himself in his study as before, but takes breaks to walk around the apartment now, or to sit down with me for coffee, or to listen to the news on the radio. But his mind, as usual, is elsewhere. No doubt he hears music in his head or is working out his ideas. I try not to interrupt him for fear of breaking his creative flow. I am happy just to have him beside me. But sometimes he can be so distracted; last week, he forgot he'd already put sugar in his coffee. I had to stop him or else he would have ended up with six teaspoonfuls of sugar. We had a good laugh about it.

Simple, lighthearted moments like this remind me of my old Herbert and our early courtship. How hesitant my parents were about his prospects! His meager salary didn't allow for any extravagance, but we were happy merely to go to Central Park or the Museum of Natural History or to Grand Central Terminal to eat sweets and people watch. We dreamed of all the places we hoped to one day visit: Boston, Philadelphia, London, Paris. And not too many years later, after we were married and his career was more established, we saw them all. I miss those carefree years, full of hope and possibility.

As much as I am happy to have John here, I think he is perhaps just a tad rigid, too bookish in his thinking. The other day, he came over to me when Herbert went for a short walk, and he told me he didn't want to worry me in any way, but that he was concerned for Herbert. He said it's likely the stress and the intensity of the work, but that Herbert has become more withdrawn and no longer gives him clear instructions. Apparently, John has spent the last few days waiting for Herbert to produce new sketches, and in the meantime, in their absence, he worked on his own music. He asked Herbert if he should leave early and come back when Herbert was ready for him, but Herbert just waved him off, and John wasn't sure how to interpret it. He said he wouldn't feel comfortable if he got paid for time he spent working on his own project. He told me Herbert has been sitting at the window, staring into the street, watching the cars pass by.

I thanked him for his honesty and concern and told him he shouldn't worry too much about it. I explained that Herbert's behavior is something to be expected, that he is an artist and that his creativity cannot be rushed or forced, and that John's role is merely to assist him, which sometimes means simply to wait patiently until he is needed. I told him to keep to his same schedule and that he is welcome to work on whatever he needs to. He apologized and repeated that he didn't mean to alarm me but that he wasn't sure what to do, since Herbert didn't want to talk at all.

If I dwelled on every time Herbert didn't want to talk to me over the years, I would have had a nervous breakdown long ago. The young man doesn't know my husband, and I am surprised that he, a composer-in-training himself, doesn't understand these things.

25

The villa was unusually quiet that morning. It looked like the others might have gone to the mainland for their day trip after all. Even Ms. Bertha was gone. All the better for Claudia, who now had the whole house to herself. Naturally, she didn't mind. She took her time at breakfast, preparing old-fashioned oatmeal with walnuts and cinnamon. Afterward, she enjoyed a leisurely cup of coffee in the art studio, taking an interest in Diego's paints. The enormous windows in this part of the house let in a soft morning light of a different hue than in her bedroom. Here it was less peachy, cooler and greener, refreshing.

Now that she was truly alone, she heard her thoughts more distinctly. Without the distraction of an Internet connection, she had been able to reach a place where she was comfortable with herself without defaulting to a pacifier, a mental white noise. She was becoming more in tune with herself, intrigued by new thoughts and ideas, growing more observant of her surroundings. She wandered around the main floor, taking note of objects she had missed before. A tall grandfather clock in the hallway, with a rotating display of day-and-night symbols. A green marble mortar and pestle on the kitchen counter. Claudia paid attention to the details, taking pleasure in allowing her mind to examine the shapes and the mechanics of various items, each one ready to dispel its secrets of function, meaning, and history.

In one of the enclosed bookcases in the office, she saw a collection of antique fountain pens displayed in a burgundy velvet box. Among them were a Pelikan, a Montblanc, a Parker, and a Waterman, all with dull bodies and nibs darkened with age. Surely these belonged to Herbert or to his wife. Claudia thought about the age before the computer and how differently previous generations of composers must have had to approach the creative process. Their sense of hearing must have been more acute. Their relationship with the ink more intimate, sacramental. She wished she could hold the fountain pens, but they were locked inside the cabinet.

The blue sky and warm temperature prompted her to bring her work outdoors. At first, Claudia thought she would sit on the veranda, but then she decided to lose herself in the woods. She picked up her portfolio and her laptop, making sure it was fully charged before she left. She took her jacket, not so much for warmth, but to serve as a blanket on which to sit. She went the opposite direction she would typically go, away from the ferry dock and the pier. She didn't have to walk far before she discovered a peaceful clearing covered in soft, lush grass. It was so clean and dry, Claudia settled right there on the ground, covering the stump in front of her with her jacket to create a makeshift desk.

Surrounded by flowering shrubbery and walnut trees, she was delighted in the beauty and harmony of her new workspace. She opened her manuscript paper and began sketching melodic lines, jotting comments above pivotal measures. Pausing every few minutes, she took a look around, listened, breathed in, and then wrote several more notes. She kept going, pushing through the mental obstacles. She wasn't particularly inspired musically, but she was determined to compose something today. Anything. A placeholder would do. She could rewrite later if needed.

She continued for half an hour, but soon her concentration wavered. Against her will and better judgment, her mind drifted to Gabriel's pronounced absence. It surrounded and enveloped her at every turn. She wasn't able to shake off the feeling. She reminisced on the handful of encounters they had enjoyed. Why did he invade her thoughts? Was it an enchantment? Infatuation? A kinship? It certainly was not love and not really a sexual attraction, and yet a throbbing ache kept tugging at her. Whatever the definition of their relationship, she was confident she would like to see him again. It might have been the feeling of ease and safety she experienced in his presence. In contrast to Victor, Diego, and Stephanie, Gabriel made her believe he genuinely cared about her welfare. He gave her reassurance without asking for anything in return. She instinctively knew that if he were still on the island right now—even if he were at the dock or in the shed, away from her—she would feel more at peace, more inspired, and more focused on her work.

How selfish of her to think this way, how possessive. She knew very little about him. She didn't remember ever asking about his family or where he was from. She naturally assumed he was a local. They had talked a bit about his interests—music, of course, woodworking, reading—but never about his past or even his present circumstances. She didn't even know where he lived. She felt guilty for never inquiring about any of these things. He seemed to her almost like a ghost who appeared and disappeared at will, without the need to eat or for a place to sleep.

A prolonged pinch inside of Claudia's stomach reminded her of lunch. She regretted not bringing any food or water with her. Even this ordinary detail reminded her of the time Gabriel took her for a boat ride, with his blue thermos and bag of sandwiches. Reluctantly, she gathered her things and headed back to the villa.

When she walked into the kitchen, Ms. Bertha was standing at the stove, pouring tea into a cup.

"Welcome, dear. Are you hungry?" She smiled at Claudia.

"Yes, I am, actually." Claudia dropped her belongings on the floor by the door.

"Here, have a seat. I'll make you a sandwich." Ms. Bertha pointed to the table with her saucer, holding the filigree porcelain teacup by its handle.

"You don't have to do it. You're so kind," Claudia answered, but pulled a chair from the table and sat down.

"It's nothing. Is ham and cheese all right with you?" She opened the refrigerator and took out deli packets, mayonnaise, and lettuce.

"Yes, thank you." Claudia was genuinely happy to be in Ms. Bertha's company. The woman was elegant and formal, yet somehow down-to-earth. "I'm sorry I haven't been very social. I should make more of an effort to come to dinner on time," Claudia said.

"Nonsense. There's no need to keep a schedule here. I know you have been working very hard." Ms. Bertha spread mayonnaise on the bread.

"You could say I'm trying to work hard." Claudia buried her face in her hands and sighed.

"How is your composition progressing? It's a cello sonata, isn't it?" Ms. Bertha asked.

"Well, no. I've decided to attempt a symphony." Claudia rose and took a teacup from the cupboard.

"I see. Writing a symphony is a worthy

endeavor. How is it coming along?"

"Not very well at the moment." Claudia turned around and leaned against the cabinet, clutching the teacup to her chest. "I'm having a hard time getting started. I guess you could say I'm scatterbrained."

"Scatterbrained? Here at Watershed?" Ms. Bertha stopped assembling the sandwich and turned to peer at Claudia. "What could possibly distract you here? Unless it's something at home?"

"I suppose I do have many things at home to keep me worried, but right now . . . I feel distracted by someone. Unsettled, I suppose." Claudia poured tea into her cup and resumed her seat.

"A man, most likely?" Ms. Bertha said, setting the sandwich on a plate.

"I don't know. I'm not even sure we are . . ." Claudia's contorted her face. She didn't know how to answer the question. "I don't think it's like that."

"Oh, dear, it's never 'like that.' Those lines are often blurred." She placed the plate with the sandwich in front of Claudia, sitting down opposite her. "Things will sort themselves out in due time. The best thing to do is to concentrate on your work." She patted Claudia's hand.

"Yes, I suppose you are right. But it's easier said than done." Claudia stared down at her meal.

"You're in the prime of your youth and your career. You should be wholeheartedly concentrated on your craft. Why allow some man to rob you of your potential? Didn't you come here to get away from it all, to give yourself the space to create something worthwhile, away from distractions?" Ms. Bertha sipped her tea.

"I feel like there's so much pulling me away from music, so much that's causing me to doubt and to procrastinate." She picked the sandwich apart, trying to decide how to handle it. "I'm sorry, I don't know anything about you or this house. Do you speak from personal experience? I mean, have you lived a creative life?" she asked.

"Yes, you could say that. I have met many artists in my lifetime. They come and go. They have various reasons and motives for stopping here. Some work methodically nonstop to produce only garbage. Others are temperamental and need space for their theatrics." She stood up, opened a cabinet, and rummaged through plastic packages until she found a box of cookies. "Others are shy and uncertain, in need of a bit of encouragement. We all have our individual paths and approaches, but what matters, in the end, is the outcome, the finished work: the symphony, the opera, the painting, the novel—whatever it is one is devoted to. Are you devoted to your art?" she asked.

"I want to be." Claudia looked away and thought for a moment. "But I'm not sure I have the strength." She turned to Ms. Bertha again. "But what about you?"

"Oh, me? I think I gave it all I had. Sometimes I

think I gave too much," she answered sternly and took a bite of a cookie. "It's difficult for me to talk about it." She pursed her lips slightly.

"I'm sorry, I didn't mean to get too personal." Claudia rested her head on her arms.

"It's all right. Whatever you do, whatever you decide about your career, your life, your symphony, do it in such a way that you have no regrets. Give it the best you have, but be smart about it," Ms. Bertha said.

"You're a wise woman, Ms. Bertha. What you're doing here is invaluable. Your work with the Foundation, opening your home to artists, your help. I've really benefited from my time here already," she said with heartfelt gratitude.

"You almost left me not too long ago." Smiling, Ms. Bertha wagged a finger at Claudia. "But I'm happy to see you've settled in nicely. It's good to have you around, dear, but I hope not to see too much of you. You keep missing dinners if you're consumed with your work. I want to take some credit for this magnificent symphony you are about to compose."

26

January 8, 1966

I have always been fearful of sudden catastrophes, unforeseen disruptions, fatal disasters. I never took into consideration that life can change gradually over time, that a tragedy can creep up unnoticed. How could I have been so blind? A crisis has unfolded in front of my very eyes, yet I didn't take note. Did I not see it? Or did I not want to see it, acknowledge it, confront it?

Doctor Ferguson was kind enough to make a private house call to examine Herbert. He asked many questions about his routine, medications, sleep patterns, workload, alcohol consumption, and such. He said he would follow up in a few weeks and keep Herbert under observation before giving his diagnosis—that it was too soon to fear anything in particular. He advised Herbert to cut down on his work hours at the school and to take a slower pace with the opera. More sleep, less stress, more walks, more green vegetables, less coffee. He patted me on the shoulder, telling me to be strong and to rise to the occasion. What a strange expression. To rise. To the occasion? Have I been sitting on my hands all this time? What occasion exactly? A singular event? The upcoming days, months, years?

What a difference a few weeks can make. Where Herbert's behavior was a bit quirky before, it is now more pronounced, even frightening. The other day, after lunch, Herbert excused himself to go to the bathroom. When he returned, he was completely undressed, save for his underwear and socks. He asked where he might find his pajamas and whether it was time for bed. He seemed utterly lost and confused, and I just sat there not knowing how to answer him. I finally gathered myself and walked back to the bathroom with him, and helped him to dress again, before suggesting he take a nap. He agreed and I led him to the sofa in his study. I left him there and went back to the kitchen to bury my face in my hands, and had a long, hearty cry. How fortunate this happened on a Sunday, so that John had not been here to see it. Now I realize what the doctor meant about rising to the occasion. I'm afraid there will be many more occasions just like this one.

I fear to give this condition its name because I feel it would be validating its existence and welcoming it into our lives. I am absolutely not ready for such a step. I will let Dr. Ferguson tell us what he needs to tell us at the right time, and not before. But Herbert's behavior does resemble Uncle Patrick's early stages of decline. It is too much to face. I need to stay strong. Perhaps this is only a temporary setback, the result of overworking and stress.

Because Herbert does continue to have good days. He still teaches, goes for walks, writes music. There are times when all is forgotten. Just two days ago, Herbert brought me flowers, and we had the most beautiful afternoon. We talked and laughed just like in the old days. He reminisced on the details of the bracelet I once lost at the British Museum in London, something I had long forgotten but for him it was as if it had happened yesterday.

But the next day he woke up confused, unable to dress himself, even though I had laid out his clothes the night before as I have done for years. He complained it was too difficult to remember which piece to put on first: the shirt, or the socks, or the pants. The immensity of the task pushed him to tears. I helped him dress and walked him to his study, where he sat in front of the window for the next few hours.

I called the school again to let them know Herbert had a cold and that he would not be coming in that day. I'm not sure how much longer I will be able to continue this deception. No one knows of our difficulties. No one at the school, none of my friends, not John, not even Herbert's sister. How do we tell them? What? When? Herbert thinks he can continue to work on the opera on his good days and simply take a break when he is not feeling like himself. He even mentioned an early retirement, but at fifty-eight, it seems quite early.

On the evening of the same day he struggled to dress himself, he experienced a window of clarity and inspiration. He kept working late into the night, and I dared not interrupt him, no matter the doctor's recommendations. I could not take it away from him. I know how strongly he feels about composing. Finishing the opera is the most important project for him right now. With the June deadline for turning in the score, before the rehearsals commence in late July, it might still be possible.

Herbert asked John if he would be available to come in as needed, without keeping a particular schedule. John, of course, agreed. He might suspect something. It was he, after all, who first brought Herbert's strange behavior to my attention, although I disregarded his concern at the time. If I had listened then, would it have made a difference? John doesn't speak to me very much. I am afraid to talk to him. Perhaps he is afraid to talk to me.

27

Over the next few days, Claudia kept to a more rigorous creative schedule. She was rising early and taking brisk morning strolls. Communing with nature in solitude did wonders for her disposition. Today, after breakfast, she spent a couple of hours browsing orchestral scores and listening to one of Schnittke's symphonies. She made notes about its movements, their structure, harmonic language, thematic ideas, the lengths of sections. Theoretically, by conducting preliminary research, she was laying the groundwork for her own symphony, but she was still far away from drafting any solid sketches of her own music. She would give herself a few more days for the score study before proceeding with her own.

The working pace was not what she had originally envisioned, but it was sensible. This was how she had approached her previous compositions, and the procedure was tried and true. Unfortunately, it looked like she would have to delay her dissertation by a few months and reschedule her defense. She didn't mind. She would need to discuss the new scenario with her advisor but didn't suppose it would be an issue for him. Greg had always supported her ideas and believed that doctoral students should pursue their own unique interests. Some of her peers had changed the focus of their research several times; she would hardly be the first.

The villa was quiet during the day, and that afternoon, Claudia enjoyed her solitary lunch and cup of tea. She sat on the veranda and watched the fluid movement of the tree canopies in the calm breeze. Her anxiety level was the lowest it had been in quite some time. She found the periods of rest therapeutic, healing, cleansing. A thought crossed her mind that if she didn't write a single line of music and instead only recuperated here, she wouldn't consider her stay at Watershed a waste. After all, this had been her intention from the beginning, but now the idea felt less frantic, more logical. Watershed seemed to be more of a peaceful sanatorium for broken artists than a creative boot camp, and this was precisely what she needed right now. She wished she had realized it sooner.

While the afternoon was warm, pleasant, and restful, the evening with its slowly setting darkness proved cold and lonely. Claudia thought she heard a conversation downstairs and left her room in search of company. The kitchen was empty, and so were the dining room and the library. She spotted a handful of scores she had left scattered on the floor beside the piano and went over to gather them and return them neatly to the shelf. She straightened the art albums on the side table and fluffed the pillows on the couch. Faint laughter drew her to the painting studio, where she found the door slightly ajar. She nudged it open to peek in.

Diego stood by the window, holding on to an easel that leaned against the wall. His raised arms firmly gripped the wooden frame. His white shirt was unbuttoned, hanging loosely around his shoulders, draping his back. His trousers, belt, and underwear were down around his ankles, exposing his hairy legs. Behind him, in a kneeling position, Victor, also shirtless, held Diego's hip with one hand, while with the other he scratched Diego's upper thigh. Victor buried his face in Diego's buttocks, biting aggressively and licking them interchangeably. Diego trembled in ecstasy, knocking the easel against the wall. The two groaned and moaned in an untamed primal duet.

Claudia stood in the doorway, holding her breath. Her arms and legs were frozen in the middle of forward momentum. The men were facing away from her so they wouldn't notice her unless she made a sound. She could still turn around quietly and leave undetected. She was discreet enough not to make a scene, to keep the discovery to herself. She didn't want any explanations or embarrassment either for them or for herself.

Like a robber careful not to trip an alarm, she began to slowly and carefully retreat, but somehow her body could not decide whether to make a left or a right turn, and she found herself trapped between the doorknob and the door frame, squirming like a moth in a spider web. The floor creaked. The door hinge shrilled.

"Shit!" she hissed to herself quietly but loudly enough to startle the men. "I'm so sorry." She looked away, waving her hands. "I didn't know. I'm just leaving. I'm really, just, please, I'm really sorry."

Diego tried to collect himself by pulling up his underwear and wrapping his shirt around his naked torso. Stumbling, his feet still caught in his pants, he rushed upon Claudia before she was able to extricate herself.

"Claudia, please, don't mention anything to Stephanie," Diego pleaded, his face painfully contorted. He rubbed his forehead and his eyes as if to sober up, to devise a plan.

"I didn't see anything. It's none of my business. I didn't mean to—" Claudia wanted to withdraw immediately, but Diego clasped her forearm.

Victor was left in the background, casually slipping on a T-shirt, watching them nonchalantly, even impatiently. Diego, now fully alert, was agitated, still clutching his unbuttoned and untucked shirt, attempting a semblance of decency.

"I beg you, Claudia, Stephanie cannot find out about this," he implored her, now tugging on her arm. "Promise me!"

"Find out about what?" asked Stephanie, who

materialized out of thin air at the door.

She pushed Claudia to the side and forced her way into the room. She looked around at the scattered paintings, Victor's exposed abdomen and ruffled hair, Diego's rumpled shirt and the pants he was attempting to zip up before he could buckle his belt.

"Oh my God! Diego! How could you? How could you do this? Anything but this!" She shoved Claudia to the side again and stormed into the corridor. The loud stomping of her high heels followed her to the front door and out of the villa.

"Stephanie!" Claudia shouted and ran after her to the veranda. She paused and looked around to determine which way the girl went. "Stephanie, wait!"

She spotted a fragment of Stephanie's silhouette running into the forest. It was already dark and difficult to see, but the light of the waning moon faintly illuminated the trees.

Claudia ran after her, across the courtyard, stumbling on the gravel. Claudia was concerned for the girl's safety, feeling it was her duty to intervene, as if Stephanie were a university student in her care. She rushed into the forest, between patches of shrubbery. Stephanie wasn't following a trail but running blindly through the wilderness. Claudia heard the villa's front door slam. Diego and Victor were following, too, or at least they were trying to figure out what was going on. She didn't glance back but ran on, bushes and brambles scratching her forearms. Low-hanging branches painfully slapped her face. Angrily, she brushed them away, but her clothing kept catching on conifers and thorns.

"Stephanie, please stop! Let's talk!" she called to the darkness, but the girl was much too quick. She could no longer see her and followed only the sound of creaking twigs and shuffling of the leaves in front of her.

"Leave me alone!" Stephanie shouted.

Good; at least now Claudia knew exactly which direction the girl was headed. She calibrated her trajectory accordingly. Stephanie wasn't too far away. The rustling of foliage ceased, and the silence suddenly gave way to a big splash. Stephanie had plunged into the river.

At once, Claudia's high school lifeguard training kicked in, and without a moment's hesitation, she jumped into the river after her.

"Come back, please—it's too dangerous!" Claudia shouted, but Stephanie was already shoulders-deep in the river and pushing farther in. Her head slipped under, and her arms waved frantically. Large air bubbles floated to the surface. Claudia dove underwater and seized the girl by the shoulders, trying to haul her to dry land. Stephanie slapped at Claudia's hands and face, but Claudia kept a firm grip. Slowly, she dragged the girl back toward the bank, until the two were safely waist-deep in river water.

"Leave me alone. I want to die!" Stephanie shouted. She was crying spasmodically and spitting out water. Her blouse was torn and her face tormented. She was convulsing, violently.

"Stephanie, please, let's get back to shore. The current is too strong here."

Sobbing, Stephanie tried to push her away, but Claudia didn't let go.

"I don't want to live. Leave me alone! You can't help me now." She was fully hysterical.

"Stephanie, please!" Claudia used all of her strength to grab the girl around the torso, blocking her arms.

"My name is not Stephanie. My name is Symphony! I have nothing to live for!" she screamed, spitting water and saliva. Her face contorted. "He doesn't love me. You're not going to compose me. Why don't you get it? You stupid bitch, you've ruined everything—can't you see that?"

Claudia let go, stunned.

"That's right, Claudia!" Victor shouted.

The men stood on the shore, staring at them and making no attempt to help.

"What's it going to take for you to get it? Why can't you just write the damn symphony?" Victor added.

"Can't you see what you have done?" asked Diego, entering the water, starting toward the women.

Stephanie quieted and crouched in the water, her face just above the surface.

"What I have done?" Claudia screamed. "Are you insane? You screw around with this girl and break her heart, and you have the audacity to tell me it's my fault?"

"Not just this. Everything is your fault." Now Victor followed Diego into the river, angrily pointing at her. "Everything here on this island is your fault. Nothing like this would have ever happened if you'd simply written the symphony like you were asked to from the beginning. How many more signs, incidents, and crises is it going to take for you to realize what you are supposed to do?"

Suddenly, Victor punched the surface of the water with his fist, and the big splash caused Claudia to cringe.

"What the hell are you talking about? What do you care what I compose or don't compose?"

She was trapped between Stephanie and the men. The full sensation of the frigid river pierced her through to the bones. She wrapped her soaked arms over her chest.

"What do I care? I couldn't care less, but, unfortunately, it all hinges on you!" Victor shouted. "Can't you see that my novel, his painting, his color blindness, her existence—everything depends on you writing this idiotic symphony?"

The bottom layers of Claudia's universe retracted, letting her slip into a dark, lonely, frightening abyss. It would be so much better not to understand what he was saying, but she understood him perfectly. And because she did, it meant she was going insane. She no longer worried about Stephanie being hysterical and out of control. She saw herself losing touch with reality.

But what exactly was reality? Her body was cold. She was shaking. She could feel the water flowing around her, pressing against her. Stephanie's weight was real, the air bubbles, the shouting. Her shoulder muscles were strained, and her hair was soaked, clinging to her face and neck. Did her senses betray her? She had heard about people suffering from schizophrenia, who reported seeing, hearing, and interacting with beings invisible to others. Was this what was happening to her just now? Had her anxiety bloomed into certifiable mental illness? She couldn't be insane! She couldn't lose control! Not like this. She would prove them wrong!

She reached out toward Stephanie and, with all the strength she could muster, grabbed her by the hair and forced her head underwater. The girl tried to fight back, to seize Claudia's arms, but instead only grasped air. She was drowning, and Claudia kept pressing down on her. Under the surface of the water, Stephanie kicked and punched with her fists against Claudia's hips.

"You want to die? Let me help you! You don't exist! I don't believe in you! Is this what you wanted? Who is insane now?" Claudia screamed.

The men grabbed for Claudia, trying to pull her away, but she resisted them, until finally, they lifted her and carried her, kicking and screaming, onto the shore. Once they shoved her onto the sand, they rushed back to pull Stephanie from the river. She was coughing and gasping for breath. Streaks of water flowed from her mouth, her nose, her hair, all down her blouse. She was choking and hyperventilating. She knelt on the sand and fell forward, her face smashing into the pebbles.

"Symphony! Are you okay, Symphony?" Diego lifted her, pulling her close to his chest, and she slipped into the cradle of his arms and legs. He patted her back and rocked her from side to side. She was breathing, but her eyes were still closed. "There you go. You'll be all right. Shh . . . everything will be all right." She coughed again, spitting more water.

Claudia watched in horror, unable to comprehend what had just happened. She lay on the ground, propped up on one elbow, panting and struggling to steady her breath. She crawled away from them in fear, and her heart pounded inside her cold chest like a bass drum. Victor stared at her with hatred and contempt. The pressure built until she could no longer suppress it, and she jumped up and ran into the forest, away from them, away from herself. She sprinted through the darkness, without any direction or plan. She needed to find something, but what exactly? What could offer her shelter? What was tangible, real, factual?

She saw a faint light from the corner of her eye. The villa. God, let it be the villa! She rushed toward it, oblivious to all obstacles in her way: the stones, the tree roots, the hanging branches, long tendrils of tall grass. She plowed through all of them, stumbling and limping, and didn't slow down until she reached the veranda.

She rushed upstairs, finding her room just as it was before. Her belongings were there. She knew them intimately and was confident they were real. She loudly dragged the desk across the floor, barricading the door. Her wet clothes clung to her body, weighing on her heavily. She tore them off frantically, hurling them to the farthest corner, as far away from herself as possible.

She ran into the bathroom and looked in the mirror above the sink. She rubbed it with both hands, as if to confirm its materiality. She did recognize her own face. Yes, it was red, scratched, and frightened, but at least it was still hers. She could hold on to this fact, make it her mental anchor.

Now completely nude, she began to slap her arms and thighs to elicit physical pain. She was glad the reaction was instantaneous. The scratches inflicted earlier by the thorns and needles were clearly visible on her forearms and hands in long punctuated streaks. She pinched and rubbed her cheeks several times, hard. She was inside, present and accounted for.

She looked around in search of familiar objects, tactile, visual proofs, but an overwhelming wave of nausea pulled her down to the floor in front of the toilet. She quickly lifted its cover and barely made it, but not in time to pull her hair away from her face. She retched and vomited so violently, in cathartic outbursts so persistent, she struggled to catch a breath. Streaks of warm tears skipped over her cheeks, dripping straight into the toilet bowl, mixing with the foul-smelling bitter chunks. Tiny freckles on her usually pale skin now transformed into the large red-and-brown blotches of strain. When her stomach was completely emptied, she fell on the floor, drew her knees to her chest, and wiped her face with her hair. She would stay right there, as long as it took. But first came the all-too-familiar shivering. In light of all this madness, it seemed strangely grounding and reassuring.

28

February 19, 1966

May God forgive me for what I have done and for what I am about to do. I condemn myself, and I absolve myself. May future generations judge me, but not until they learn about my predicament and my motives.

I always believed there was right and wrong, good and evil, Heaven and Hell, honesty and deceit. Now I am no longer sure. Now I think there are necessary sacrifices that increase the likelihood of survival—that the greater good trumps smaller, less consequential choices, however questionable.

Herbert is on a leave of absence from the school, per Dr. Ferguson's orders and is mostly confined to the apartment. Even though his confused episodes do not happen too often, they are unpredictable and difficult to conceal. It seems better to withdraw from public life, to limit the chances of humiliation. After another one of his outbursts, Herbert dismissed John altogether. He told me the opera was nearly finished, so there was no need for outside help anymore. He insisted he could finalize his own orchestrations, that the most strenuous work was behind him. For the entire week, he continued to compose on his own, and I dared not question him. He seemed to be in good spirits, his old music-possessed self.

Then, one day, I thought I would check on him in his study. I found him at his desk, crying, scribbling something awfully incoherent, pressing on the fountain pen nib so hard that he deformed it beyond repair, causing the ink to spill onto the cuff of his shirt. I wanted to console him but didn't know what to say. He seemed cognizant and able to think clearly, but he told me the music had left him, that it was beyond his capacity.

What was I to do? Was I to sit and watch this man unravel before my eyes? Should I have allowed this opera, this crowning achievement of his career, to fade away and never be heard? Should I have let this great composer be brushed aside, disposed of, relegated to the past? No! As his wife, as his guardian and helper, as a lover of music, as a steward of his legacy, I knew what I needed to do.

I had the hardest time tracking down Rita. I scoured Herbert's address books for her telephone number, but the only contact information he had was long out of date. I asked about her at the school through some back channels so as to not to draw too much suspicion. I was finally able to get in contact with another student of Nadia Boulanger who knew of Rita's whereabouts. She was employed, just as I had sadly predicted, by a secretarial agency downtown.

I asked her to meet me at Bemelmans without giving her an explanation, and she reluctantly obliged. I'm not sure why I chose the piano bar. It was the middle of the day, so no one would be playing at that time anyway. Maybe because subconsciously I didn't want Herbert to find us—he never would set foot in such a place—not that he would follow me now. Or maybe because I just wanted a drink. The dimness of the room was a welcome relief, but the Madeline murals put me in a mood of instant nostalgia for my long-passed youth. Though, I hardly needed the world to remind me of impermanence of all things.

Rita was in a state of her own. She looked pale, a bit thinner than before, and the quality of her modest beige suit did not complement her in the slightest. I ordered a round of martinis for us, midday or not, and she didn't protest. She was visibly upset when I told her about Herbert's condition. I asked for her help. Nothing specific because, truth be told, I didn't know what to ask for. She agreed to come to the apartment to take a look at the score so I could understand the scope of the work still left to be done.

She came over the following evening, and Herbert was delighted to see her. He greeted her as if no time had passed since they were last together. I could tell she was glad to see him, though she was, understandably, restrained. He excused himself, went to the living room, and turned on the radio to listen to music! (These days it is so hard for me to discern anymore what is normal for him and what is not.)

Rita and I stepped into his study, and I handed her the Iphigenia *score. She began flipping through the manuscript, ordering the pages on the floor, and sorting them into several piles. She caressed the paper and at times covered her mouth to pause and think. She was so absorbed by the process, she may have forgotten I was sitting right beside her, watching her.*

"Here is the section I orchestrated for him," she said, gently, and kept going forward through neatly written passages. After she turned many pages, the handwriting changed, and I supposed it must have been John's. She kept reading through it, nodding along. Then she stopped and went back a few passages, then ahead again, as if searching for something. She continued further forward and burst into tears. She said this section was complete nonsense, irreparable gibberish, that it would need to be replaced in its entirety. That it was not even a sketch or an idea, but something inarticulate. She kept crying and apologizing, and I tried to quiet her, but she was beside herself. I had to be firm, and I told her to get a hold of herself and tell me about the overall progress of the work and whether anything might be done to see it through to fruition.

I could not be more devastated when she showed me that only about fifty percent of the score was viable, up to the point where John had ceased his orchestration, and even that section seemed much weaker than what she remembered Herbert had produced before. She was so frantic, she excused herself and abruptly left the apartment, leaving me there all alone and helpless. I was losing Herbert, that much I knew, but now I was also losing his music, this opera. The entire world was turning away from us, leaving us in the midst of a menacing silence. It was cruel and grotesque. I couldn't breathe. I wanted to scream, but I had no air left in my lungs.

Two days later, Rita telephoned to apologize for her emotional behavior, and we agreed to meet again at the Peacock in Greenwich Village for coffee. It was closer to where she now lived and less conspicuous for me. It was widely known Rita had worked for Herbert in the past but some people might think it strange for me to meet her alone like this. I didn't want to chance it.

I have no idea if she suspected that which I was about to propose, but it didn't take long to convince her. I told her I knew of no one else to whom Herbert would have wanted his music entrusted. That if she refused, I would understand. But if she agreed, I would not judge her motives. That we both would do it for Herbert and his legacy. She cried again, and I cried with her, for her, for him, and for myself. What a strange, unexpected camaraderie with this woman I once derided.

I can't honestly tell what she once felt for Herbert, if anything at all. Perhaps it truly was only respect and admiration. And if they were once feelings of romantic love, they cannot remain the same now. But I would be ignorant to think she agreed solely for Herbert's sake. I may not be a composer or a performer, but I have been an observer of Herbert's world long enough to understand that finishing this opera was most likely Rita's only chance to have her music heard on this scale. Yes, I am fully aware when I write "her music." If she is to finish the work properly, she has no choice but to compose new passages entirely of her own design. And this does not sadden or trouble me. I feel instinctively that this is what Herbert would have wanted.

29

Claudia slept more soundly that night than ever before. It was the slumber of a boulder or a dead person. One in which all cares are obliterated, all counters reset, all pain receptors anesthetized. She couldn't remember how or when she got into bed and was surprised to wake up under the plush soft covers, warm and rested. It was still dark outside, likely very early morning. She had lost all sense of time. Unable to return to sleep, she switched on her bedside lamp and sat up, looking around the room. Her clothes were scattered everywhere. The desk still barricaded the door. She recalled last night's events, but they now seemed to float in a more distant, hypothetical space.

She felt a sudden wave of energy, a restlessness that forced her to stand up and pace the floor. It was not a physical desire to run or to exercise, but a strong emotional urge to unburden her mind. Her neurons danced inside her brain, sparking off against her skull. She wanted to scream, like during a panic attack, except this time the internal tension demanded a different outlet. She could not sit still, so she tried to distract herself with any physical activity she could think of. She flipped through the nightstand drawer. She walked back and forth. She went into the bathroom and shuffled through her cosmetics bag. She wasn't looking for anything. She merely needed to keep her hands occupied. She returned to her room, to straighten her bed covers. She abandoned the task.

She found in her suitcase a sweater and a pair of pants and dressed quickly. She picked up her wet clothes from the floor and carried them to the bathroom, throwing them in the tub. She paced some more until finally dropping down at her desk. It didn't matter that it was pushed against the door. She waited there in half darkness, trying to calm her restless mind. She knew what to do next.

She brought over the nightstand lamp, placing it on the tabletop, and gathered the scattered manuscript. It took her a while before she found all her pens, pencils, and erasers, which had rolled across the floor in all directions. She laid everything on the desk. Leaning with her palms flat on the wooden surface, she closed her eyes, inhaled, and exhaled slowly, deeply.

Without thinking, she reached for the fountain pen. It was not usually her tool of choice, especially not for the initial sketch, but she obeyed her instincts. She quickly drew music clefs up and down all the staves on the page, assigning system brackets to group the families of instruments. It would be too soon to appoint each instrument its individual line.

Instead, she would follow a shortcut, clustering all strings together, all woodwinds together, all brass, and all percussion. Without any hesitation, she marked the time signature and the tempo at the top of the page. "Allegro Moderato." No; she scratched it frantically. No more Italian pretentiousness. She was an American. "Mid Tempo, quarter note equals seventy."

She began writing in entire phrases. She thought she would fill in the background and middle layers later, but then found herself notating everything as she moved forward, without stopping. Years of grueling ear training, score study, focused listening, and analysis now paid dividends in effortless, uninterrupted self-expression. She threw entire gestures, entire shapes onto the page. She then molded, ornamented, and sculpted them to her liking. She began with a slow motive in the upper register of the violoncellos, reminiscent of Brahms, but uniquely of her own creation. She underpinned it with the French horn and the violas. Other instruments joined and wove in one by one in a swell of slowly rising tension. There was no detectable pulse in the music, only a wave of sound gradually but incessantly pushing the silence away.

What would the music be about? This question, whose answer was usually a prerequisite before Claudia could write anything, now seemed a futile exercise. The music would be about everything. It would be about her, and it would be about itself. About wanting to be written, about being afraid to be written. About being and ceasing, about wanting to live but seeking death, about loneliness, fear, anxiety, panic, struggle, loss, hope, light, the rawness of life, honesty, sacrifice. She would compose for herself but also for Rita, for Herbert, and his wife. Something deep inside of her felt their loss and wanted to give it a voice. She owed it to them, to herself, to all the others whose music was ever muted, rejected, suppressed. She needed to express all the emotions welling up in her since her arrival at Watershed: her self-doubt, her uncertainties about her career and her life choices, her mental struggles, her interactions with Victor, Diego, Symphony, Gabriel—everything having a category and a label, and everything unspoken, intangible, supernatural, or inexplicable.

Had her anxiety skyrocketed into full-blown paranoia? Was she certifiably delusional? These questions were irrelevant. Words and linguistic definitions were inadequate, constraining. Another language altogether was needed to convey her experiences. And she discovered this secret language at the core of her being. Though she heard it for the very first time, it was the most familiar and natural essence of her. It flowed out of her, into the air, surrounded her, wrapped itself around her arms, chest, and legs. It radiated in multiple branches, tender shoots, soft twigs. It carried her effortlessly, read and spoke her mind in colorful outbursts, in rugged textures, in wavy and jagged lines. Whatever it was, whatever she was, she wished she could inhabit it indefinitely, no matter the cost. This was better than alcohol, food, love, sex, or any intellectual high.

The wall of sound kept pushing against her, stronger and faster than she could notate it. Her handwriting was erratic and hurried. Instead of round, filled shapes for the note heads, she was now marking off squiggly check marks. She slanted the note masts and beams in whatever direction was fastest at the moment. She didn't even use musical notes to record certain passages. Instead, she drew in cryptic symbols, angled lines, arrows, solid blocks, spirals.

Now the music erupted in pointillist splotches, forming a mesh of individual sounds hanging in the air and twinkling like distant city lights at nighttime. The bass clarinet came to the foreground, and so did the oboe, muted trumpet, and pizzicato violins. The cacophony kept morphing through various instrumental combinations, traveling through several registers. It grew, faded, grew again, paused, and came back, alive again, and with more force.

The auditory experience blended with visual cues. Claudia saw the music the way she sometimes did in her dreams. Colorful patterns came floating toward her, and she, with the power of her mind and her pen, as its extension, was channeling them into new configurations, new sequences, relationships, pairings, flavorings. No emotion could not be expressed through the music. They were all subjective, autobiographical. She stood in the midst of them, naked and vulnerable, effortlessly juggling them in three-dimensional arrays.

She recalled the feud between Brahms and Liszt, who stood on opposite ends of the argument of whether music should remain an absolute, pure form, inexpressible through words, or if it should be programmatic, describing specific textual and poetic ideas, following a plot. Half a dozen modern essays about the insufficiency of music to express particular emotions without the aid of another art form flashed before her eyes. In her career, she had been the one to study and argue these concepts in depth. And now she could prove their futility with a simple movement of her fountain pen. She was transfixed into a new reality, one that existed above trivial considerations. None of them mattered now. What mattered was to be inside the music. To simply be music. She understood perfectly why Symphony wanted to be written. Now Claudia wanted to be written, to become the Symphony herself.

She didn't feel hunger. How liberating it was not to need to pause for a meal. When she was thirsty, she simply darted to the bathroom and drank directly from the faucet above the sink. Then she immediately ran back to continue where she had left off, hoping to be able to keep up. The sun rose and traveled the entire arc of the sky. She kept going late into the night until she finally collapsed, asleep again. A day passed, maybe two, perhaps a week. She didn't know for sure and didn't care. She only cared that the music persisted. She would remain inside it as long as it took, as long as she physically could.

30

March 21, 1966

Rita has been with us these past three weeks. She does go home in the evenings, of course, but is here, in the apartment, most of the rest of the day. Because she needs to fully focus on the opera, I asked her to quit her job, and I offered her a generous weekly stipend. I don't want her to worry about money right now, and besides, the woman deserves to be compensated for her talent, and yes, for her silence and sacrifice.

While I did have some hesitation before she began, it quickly dissipated. It would not be in her interest to reveal our plan to anyone. It certainly would not help her reputation as an aspiring composer, and I could always deny her claims by saying she worked the entire time off Herbert's sketches. But I'm sure it will never come to that.

This is how I see it: It is an arrangement benefiting everyone involved. The project will bring her invaluable experience, and she will be able to hear her work performed by a full orchestra, soloists, and a chorus. Objectively speaking, Iphigenia *is still Herbert's opera. It was his idea to begin with. If half of it has already been written, then I assume Rita will base the remaining sections on the existing passages, imitating his style.*

I asked her not to take any portions of the manuscript home with her and to only work on it in our apartment. Obviously, I can't make her sign any legal agreements, but at least I can control the physical whereabouts of the score.

She comes in around nine, after breakfast, leaves for a short break around noon, and continues to write until five or six, often stretching even beyond seven or eight in the evening. Sometimes I bring her a cup of coffee or a snack. I don't attempt to curb the intensity of her work. For now, I am merely here to support her, so she can produce the finest music possible. If she is fatigued, she doesn't show it. She keeps quiet in Herbert's study, occasionally checking her writing on the piano or by humming. Every now and then, I hear her muttering something to herself, mostly the passages of the libretto or random Italian musical terminology.

Having resigned most of my social activities, I stay in the apartment with Herbert to be on hand when his symptoms reappear. His behavior can be either unstable and incomprehensible or, at other times, perfectly rational and agreeable. I try to take him for daily walks around the city. Visiting various landmarks brings back his memories, and I sense it reassures him. An alley in Central Park where we fed the pigeons; a diner where, during our early years, we once had a lunch of only coffee and toast; the view of the East River—all these remind him of our life together, the period of time still very much alive in his mind. He remembers minute, unexpected details from the past, yet today he keeps asking me when we'll eat lunch after I've already told him four times that we ate two hours ago.

I never fully know what he is thinking or how lucid he is. Sometimes it seems he understands why Rita is here and wholeheartedly approves, and at other times I detect a certain sadness and restlessness in him. We have never truly discussed her purpose here. I only ever talk about Rita "helping" him but never mention the missing music or the money changing hands. I think that on his good days, he realizes what she is doing and doesn't want to agitate me beyond what I have to endure already. Perhaps he is making peace with it.

Yesterday, he spent time with Rita in the study. She moved to the side table while he took his desk. He was scribbling something, but I was afraid to ask about it. I caught Rita's eye when I passed by. Without words, we instinctively conveyed to each other that we should both let him be. He continued that way for quite a long time, while Rita composed beside him.

Later that evening, after she was gone and Herbert was in the sitting room, I entered the study to retrieve his notes. There, on a sheet of staff paper, he'd written random letters and numbers in crooked rows. Many of the symbols were only partially formed, with some devolving into doodles and unintelligible markings, almost as if a preschooler had attempted to copy an adult's writing. But he didn't seem upset, and all day had remained quiet and content. I wasn't about to probe him about it.

The other day, Lenny telephoned unexpectedly with

changes he wanted to incorporate into one of the arias, asking if he could come over to discuss them. The prospect terrified me. I told him that Herbert and I had a prior engagement but that Rita, his assistant, would take notes and that Herbert would get back to him later. Naturally, I took Herbert for a walk before Lenny arrived and let Rita handle everything. We averted a crisis, but for how much longer? We are walking on thin ice. Only five months remain before rehearsals commence. The entire score and all the parts for soloists, chorus, and instrumentalists, along with the piano reductions, have to be ready by then. I dread what will happen. I'm sure the conductor will want Herbert to attend the rehearsals. How are we going to manage it?

Yesterday, Herbert was unusually agitated. He insisted John has stolen his manuscripts and demanded I call the police immediately. I reminded him that John has been gone for six weeks now and that he could have no reason to steal anything. Herbert raised his voice at me and told me that John came in the middle of the night and ransacked his study, that he took all his books, letters, and all of his music. Of course, none of it was true, but I had no way of arguing with him. I wanted to walk him to his study to show him that everything was as before, but he told me to leave him alone, that I was conspiring with John to defraud him. That word, "defraud," frightened me and left me speechless, but, thankfully, Herbert walked away and, in a few minutes, forgot all about being upset.

Yet I was left restless afterward, thinking incessantly

on this horrible word. Was I defrauding Herbert? Was I defrauding Rita, myself, the opera company? Was Rita defrauding us? Later, I asked how she felt about our arrangement and what she wanted to do when this was over. She said she wasn't sure, that this situation was not anything she had ever anticipated, and it was difficult to make any plans for the future since the opera was all-consuming. She told me that once you have worked on such a grand project, it is a challenge to return to small pieces of chamber music. That the rush one gets from gigantic sounds and forms is a highlight of one's creative output, and it's hard to replicate it with anything else. She doubted she could ever, under her own name, attain the recognition required to secure such projects and that she was enjoying the moment while she could, without obsessing about the future.

I realize this aspect is the most difficult for her. To be so close to something she loves so dearly, yet unable to attain it. Perhaps this is the cruelest of life's tricks. But this is something we both entered into willingly, fully aware of the limitations and possible consequences. Deep down, I do hope it will somehow be to her benefit. I truly wish her success with her own music and happiness in her personal life. She strikes me as a worthy young woman with much talent and sensitivity. There is no doubt in my mind she would get very far with her ability if only she'd been born a man.

No, I do not feel that I am defrauding anyone. It is Herbert's illness that has defrauded all of us. It is this life, with all its brutal and unexpected blows. This is the hand we were dealt, and we are playing the game to the best of our abilities.

31

Now that Claudia had completed the first sketch of her symphony, her work style and pace were changing and, consequently, she was coming down from the initial high. It wasn't that she was less inspired, but that she had switched her focus from capturing and reveling in the ideas to developing and molding them. She put aside the emotional approach in favor of the analytical one. She now spent her time examining her melodic lines, harmony, texture, pacing, and instrumentation as they fit within shorter fragments and as they related to each movement and to the whole. This stage was no less exciting, but far from the original euphoria. Claudia was more grounded now, more methodical, more perceptive and detail oriented. She spent much time polishing elements she had been forced to lay aside in the beginning. She played with moving around entire sections, finding surprising and thrilling sonic combinations. She transposed smaller segments, inverted them, truncated or elongated them. No experiment was off limits.

She continued to work in her room but also

returned to walking outside. This time, instead of the relaxing nature strolls, she took long power walks during which she incessantly mulled over her musical ideas. She was oblivious to her surroundings. No longer interested in the river, the trees, the grass, the insects, or the birds, she plowed on, unwavering in her focus, the ground beneath her feet having become an intellectual treadmill. The rhythm of walking energized the body and the brain.

At first, when Claudia had been so intensely concentrated on her symphony, she hadn't given much thought to the events that had pushed her over the edge. But now that she was feeling stable, it was time to face some fundamental questions. Namely, "Who are the fellow artists on the island?" and "How should she relate to them?" No one had reached out to her or interrupted her when she was preoccupied with her work, but now she was beginning to hear them moving around the house and the outdoors. On occasion, she saw Symphony from the window. The girl seemed to be healthy and quite happy. Her new favorite pastime was sitting on a blanket at the forest edge, reading or doodling in a notebook. But Claudia wasn't ready to reestablish contact with her and hoped Symphony would keep away. Diego was coming and going from the villa with his portable easel, a stretched canvas, a paint-splashed toolbox, and a folding stool. He was usually gone all day and returned only when the daylight dissipated. Victor was around but stayed indoors, wrapped up in his novel, and Claudia managed to avoid him as well.

There was absolutely no question that Watershed was a supernatural place. She thought about all the conversations and bizarre events leading her (and yes, forcing her) to write this symphony. She was aware that in their absence she would never have attempted such a monumental undertaking. And then, of course, the work itself, pages upon pages of music of such intensity and quality as she had never dreamed of writing before. The symphony itself was the most persuasive evidence of having encountered something magical, life-altering. Seeing it in front of her, notated on music staves, securely lodged in her memory and playable at will in her head, she treasured it above any other thing material or immaterial, any conviction, experience, or instinct. Put simply: she had groundbreaking music in her hands and didn't care how she had gotten it, whether through the power of her intellect, supernatural forces, or mental illness.

But no, she was not crazy! Crazy people did not write music of this caliber. Yet, a small part of her was aware that she wasn't quite sane either. She was somehow balancing on a razor's edge between the two states. Still, she wouldn't dare to name or categorize her fellow artists—these characters, these beings. She saw what they were helping her accomplish, she knew the effects of their influence, but whether they were objectively real or products of her imagination, ghosts, phantoms, visions, angels, manifestations, or spirits, was yet to be determined.

Claudia noticed another significant shift in herself. Although her usual anxiety came and went as before, she found a small kindling of light drawing her toward life. Her thoughts no longer drifted toward self-destruction. She no longer imagined or hoped for death. The symphony gave her a definite and immediate purpose. She had a reason to get up in the morning, to stay focused and productive. It caused her to look forward to the future. She felt responsible for the music and wanted to see it to fruition.

Still, the issue of her violent behavior toward Symphony remained, and Claudia wondered how she should handle it. An apology would probably be in order, a remorseful gesture. And how should she behave around the others? They seemed to have forgotten about that frightful night. No one had called the police. No one had forced her to leave. She decided to wait for the right time to attempt reconciliation. But to ask them about their nature? To tell them she knew? Would that not be a little awkward?

But what if she was wrong about them? What if she was the only sane one of the bunch? The more she thought about it, the more plausible it seemed.

She could have arrived at the music on her own. It happened. Composers were struck by lightning before. The symphony had most likely been locked inside of her, waiting to be brought out at the right moment.

So, she had an altercation with a girl, in the river. So what? Women can be emotional and temperamental. They can be triggered. And the others? They had acted out some fantasy, pressed her sensitive buttons, playing with her, entertained themselves at her expense.

Things were clear one minute and obscure the next. It was no use trying to figure it out in one sitting. The more she attempted to understand it, the further away she felt from the music. In time it would all sort itself out, but for now the symphony must remain a priority. It was the only thing she did not doubt or question.

32

August 12, 1966

I absolutely dreaded the read-throughs and the proper opera rehearsals. How would we manage with Herbert? There were a couple of times in the theater when I sensed the imminent onset of his symptoms, forcing us to withdraw quickly under the guise of a fever, or indigestion, or whatever came to mind. With Herbert's leave of absence from the school, it is widely known he is having health problems. I think people may suspect cancer or some other serious illness, but no one dares to ask outright.

The opera company has not been too demanding of his time. Rita, as his official assistant, is in charge of overseeing the score during rehearsals and answering any questions the conductor or the chorus master might have. But so far, it looks to me like they are finding their way around without her help. Still, with her there as Herbert's proxy, his absence is less glaring. Officially, she is there to communicate all questions to him. Unofficially, she makes all the required changes to the score herself and brings them back to the next rehearsal as if they came from Herbert.

Henrietta Rudolphi, an alto, who plays the role of Artemis, had the audacity to ask Herbert to rewrite one of her arias this late in the project. She complained that her warm lower register didn't receive enough exposure during the performance. She kept apologizing and babbling on about what she believed Artemis should sound like and how she felt compelled to follow her artistic integrity. She said she was sidelined by Iphigenia, a soprano, whose arias appear more vibrant and spectacular, and broke down crying at Herbert's feet. She was so beside herself, she couldn't stop her shtick, and left in a hurry before either of us could respond to her complaints. Within two days, Rita had the aria completely reworked without too many instrumental changes and Henrietta was overjoyed, blowing kisses to Herbert from the stage.

I can tell what a great satisfaction it is for Herbert to hear his music performed. And even during Rita's passages, he seems deeply moved. Still, I detect a certain powerlessness in him, a pain, or restlessness. But maybe I am imagining these things because I cannot truly know what is going through his mind anymore and whether or not he can process the music he hears the way he used to. I want to believe he can, but a logical part of me knows he can't. If he cannot or can only partially, what is it that he hears? What are those sounds to him? Something merely familiar, or something still intellectually and aesthetically stimulating? To what degree? I fear even on his good days, this ability is greatly reduced. My heart breaks for him. How cruel is this incurable disease!

I would be remiss if I didn't mention the new auditorium. It is a sight to behold, and not in a good way. I am told the audience capacity is comparable to what we had at the Old Met building. But there are no traditional carvings and less gold all around, though at least they made an allowance for a gold damask curtain. They wanted nothing to do with the old world, they said. All must be new, new, new! Oh, the never-ending progress. As a token of remembrance, they allowed crystal chandeliers, both in the lobby and the theater. They are reminiscent of my favorite Old Met starburst, though these have satellite moons and look more futuristic. Everything seems more modern and cold with the Italian marble and concrete. I don't think I will ever get used to it. At least the auditorium itself is still paneled in exotic wood and not glass or some dreadful metal, or else the building would have failed utterly. I suppose it could be worse. At least we didn't get a spiral ramp like the atrocious Guggenheim's. I am too old-fashioned for all these modernisms. I feel I can't keep up with the world, rushing ahead of us, leaving us behind.

33

The next few days were unusually warm. Claudia moved her desk back to the window again, where she could enjoy the view of the greenery and the foliage newly changing color. But the extraordinary pace of her work was taking its toll, tiring her mind, and she desperately needed to quiet her incessant thoughts. Having tidied her room and completed a few basic chores, she brought her tea out onto the veranda in search of a tranquil moment. The imminent sunset caused the forest to glow in sepia and red. As she settled on the bench and began to sip the amber liquid, Diego entered the courtyard from the thicket behind the shed, carrying his portable easel, toolbox, and canvas. Though he was all smiles, he moved slowly and seemed worn out.

"The light was spectacular today," he said, as he approached the veranda.

"Looks like you've been working hard. Are you painting again?" Claudia inquired, keeping her distance.

"Yes, my color perception came back. I can't tell you what a great feeling it is. It's like I'm seeing color for the first time. I just can't get enough of it!" He dropped his toolbox onto the porch, gesticulating with excitement. His shirt was splattered with green-and-blue paint and his pants were splotched muddy brown where he had dried off his brushes. "I'm painting the river this week. Here, take a look."

Claudia rose from the bench and walked closer to the canvas he held in front of him.

"Of course, it's not finished, but I think I'm finally getting somewhere."

He swung the canvas around so he could glance at it, and then displayed it again. Claudia bent slightly to take in the details. She was astounded at the abundance of color. He had stayed away from harsh and glaring pigments, preferring a subdued palette instead, but the wealth of the intermediate hues made the scene vibrant and expansive. The river seemed especially alive. He broke the greens with ultramarine and umber in such a subtle way, she could almost smell the water on the canvas. Tiny specks of titanium white, placed sparingly in strategic places, infused the painting with wild energy. Claudia was in awe. She enjoyed his monochromatic pencil sketches, but this painting was pure poetry.

"This is phenomenal, Diego! You are good! What are you going to title this one?" she asked excitedly.

"I'm not sure. What do you think?"

" 'The Flow.' No question about it."

Enchanted, she took a couple of steps backward to gain a wider perspective and then returned closer.

"That's a good title," Diego agreed. "All I can say is, thank you for writing the Symphony. You don't even realize what a difference you have made." He smiled tranquilly at her.

"I'm not sure I understand everything that has happened since . . . you know . . . 'the breakdown,' shall we call it?" She didn't look him in the eyes, struggling to find the right words.

"Oh, I think you do understand." He rested his canvas against the railing and stood opposite her, unencumbered. "You have finally found your sweet spot, and that affected everyone around you. This is what we were waiting and hoping for all this time. So yes, thank you."

She wasn't returning his gaze, so he leaned in to elicit a reaction from her.

"Yes, I can see that, but I don't understand the mechanics of it, you know?" she said impatiently, and finally looked up. "I mean, how does the symphony cause you to regain your color perception?"

"Who cares about the mechanics? Watershed has a rare vibe. People come here for one reason only: to find their creative muse. You must have heard this before you came?"

"Not really. I was accepted to the program at the last minute, and, honestly, I didn't have much time to research it," Claudia replied.

"It doesn't matter. Consider yourself lucky. There are so many artists out there who wish they could be in your shoes." He knelt down and rummaged inside his toolbox. "Everyone wants to find the holy grail, the creative flow, the recipe. So, you found it. Just enjoy it for what it is, without trying to get it patented. Sometimes I think the less we understand, the better."

"Yes, but why does what I do affect you and the others?" She leaned on the railing and relaxed. He didn't exhibit any ill feelings toward her.

"I'm not sure. I wish I had a better answer for you. All I know is, my eyesight was deteriorating, but your music allowed me to see in color again. I don't remember ever painting with this level of hunger."

He took out a piece of cloth and cleaned a hardening blob of black paint from a palette knife. Claudia noticed Symphony waving at her from the edge of the forest, enjoying the remnants of sunlight. Claudia waved back but was still too apprehensive to approach her.

"Have the two of you reconciled?" she asked Diego, nodding inconspicuously toward Symphony.

"Yes, we have. But it's clear we will never be together again. I am not the right man for her, and she knows that." He picked up his toolbox and canvas. "And I don't feel so bad, knowing she got what she came to Watershed for. Maybe it was meant to happen this way. It's for the best."

He motioned for Claudia to help him with the door; she held it wide open and followed him inside. She returned her cup to the kitchen, exchanging a soft smile with Ms. Bertha, who was folding sheets in the laundry room across the hallway. Diego had gone to the art studio, and Claudia went in search of him. His explanation of their situation intrigued her, and she wanted more. Inside the studio, Victor was hunched over his laptop, his paper notes scattered across the table. Seeing Claudia, he raised his arms and yawned, clenching and unclenching his fists. He looked tired.

"Did you sleep at all last night? You look terrible," Claudia said.

"Thanks a lot." He smirked. "No, I didn't sleep, actually. The writing was too good. All my twists have finally paid off." He stood up and began to pace, stretching his stiff legs. "I wasn't sure I would be able to pull it off, but it all came together." He rubbed his hands and then ran them through his messy hair. He raised his eyebrows and opened his eyes as wide as he could, trying to stay awake. "I think the hardest part is behind me. All that's left is the third and final act."

"What are you planning for it?" Claudia asked, carefully, uncertain if he still resented her.

"You'll have to hang around to see for yourself. I don't know yet." He sat down on the couch and leaned back with his hands clasped behind his neck.

Claudia took the chair nearby. "Are you following a standard arc of a suspense thriller?" She wanted him to know she wasn't entirely ignorant about his profession.

"No, not really. It's not so much a whodunit but more about the characters finding themselves in various contexts, about the readers suspending their disbelief. It's a journey between the real and the supernatural."

"So, it is supernatural?" she asked, gaping at him, awaiting a more definite answer, a clue, a hint.

"It depends on how you look at it. My characters travel seamlessly between the two, and we never know which is which. That's kind of the point, to never be sure."

"Fascinating. So where do you find the inspiration for your plots, Victor?" Claudia hoped he would shed more light on their predicament.

"Inspiration,"—he scoffed—"is a concept for amateur bloggers. The plots are everywhere. They hide in objects around us. In this house, in Ms. Bertha, in Diego, in you and me. You can pluck them up at any moment and mold them to your liking. Isn't that how you compose your music?"

"Not usually . . ." She paused and gave it some thought. "But the last two weeks have been different for me. Yes, you could say the music was pouring in from my surroundings, from myself. For once, I didn't need external ideas. I was notating it as it was coming at me." Claudia undulated her arms to form a crashing wave.

"Well, there you go. It has been the same for me. Maybe not initially, but after the drama with Symphony, when you finally started to compose, things took off."

"Claudia, you're the woman of the hour!" Diego roared.

"No, you're the woman of the week—of the month!" Victor countered, high-fiving her.

She stared at them, bewildered.

"I don't know about that. I'm not going to take credit for any wacko happenings on this island." She laughed nervously. "But whatever did happen, I'm glad we all managed to find our muses."

"Don't be so modest, Claudia. You are our muse!" Diego beamed, stretching his arms toward her.

"No, I don't consent to it. Keep me out of it." She grinned, raising her hands in surrender. "I'm sure you would be doing just fine without my antics." She was pleased, though, that she had somehow patched up the relationship and decided to leave it at that. Now didn't seem the right time, after all, to start asking strange questions.

34

September 16, 1966

Iphigenia *was stunning. The New Met at Lincoln Center is magnificent. I have no words to express how fantastic was the spectacle the opera company put on to stage the premiere. The soloists, the chorus, the orchestra, the costumes, the wigs, the props, the choreography, the new motorized stages and hydraulic elevators—all perfectly in concert to form an unforgettable production.* The Old Met, *in comparison, was practically a puppet show. This building is all that was promised and more. I take back everything critical I ever said about modern architecture. When I first took a backstage tour during a rehearsal, I thought the rigging system and the coulisses were overdone and the space too extravagant, but now I see the architects were right in investing so much in them. The depth of the stage made an enormous impact from the audience, and the colorful layered screens and dissolving lights were absolutely ethereal.*

I was moved to tears by the first act and could hardly contain myself during the second. Herbert and I spent the third act backstage in anticipation of his curtain call. I hoped and prayed this simple task would go well for him, and it did, even though he walked slowly and with the help of a cane. He didn't wave or smile, but it doesn't matter—we could blame it on a composer's persona or stage fright. Just as long as he was able to walk by himself from here to there and back without incident. I bawled my eyes out as everyone congratulated me and expressed admiration for Herbert.

Yes, I was there to celebrate his music, but when all was over, all the other emotions plaguing me came crashing down. Somehow, we made it through this ghastly time and were able to bring Iphigenia *to her premiere, but now the gravity of what I have endured—what I must still endure—has squeezed all the life right out of me. It was Herbert's goodbye to the opera, and mine as well. This world that gave us purpose and that supported us for all these years is not ours to claim forever. We stood among all the crew and singers, all the commotion and euphoria, knowing full well these would soon recede from us, that in the end, our colleagues would abandon and replace us. I thought I would faint. I don't remember how we returned home, except that Rita hailed us a taxi. Everything else is a blur.*

A few days later, the paper reviews came in, and I began to collect all the clippings.

"Herbert Anders, without timidity or second-guessing, has shown the audience what a seasoned, confident composer is capable of . . ."

"Magnificent mastery of the dramatic medium. A seamless marriage of the libretto and the music carrying and supporting it effortlessly yet creating its own depth

and meaning. . ."

"Iphigenia *is a triumph of Gesamtkunstwerk, with a seamless, all-encompassing experience . . .*"

"*As the opera progresses, it keeps opening new sonic strata. The third act especially brought coloristic approaches unheard of before in America, perhaps even in Europe. One can only hope we hear more music from the groundbreaking genius of Herbert Anders . . .*"

"*Herbert Anders is worthy of the title of 'Great American Composer.' His music, inevitably, will be remembered for centuries to come. The Metropolitan Opera made a very wise choice in commissioning this work. Let us hope that more of his productions will be staged in the near future . . .*"

"Iphigenia *performances are sold out for the next five weeks, and the Metropolitan Opera anticipates its run will be extended as interest in the work grows . . .*"

"*No longer second-class to European opera, American stage now has her own hero in the composer Herbert Anders.*"

The very same day, the telephone started ringing with interview requests. I spoke to a few reporters but then stopped answering entirely, and the next day I unplugged the telephone from the wall. We must leave the city for a while. Herbert and I need a hiding place. With the few scattered moments we have left, I want us to spend them in the house that has always brought us tranquility and happiness. Our luggage is all packed. First thing tomorrow morning, we will be on our way to Watershed.

When Herbert and Lenny first discussed the libretto

of Iphigenia, *they couldn't agree on the ending. There are different versions of the myth. In some, she is rescued by Artemis, and in others, she is sacrificed. Herbert, the eternal optimist, wanted the opera to be uplifting and triumphant, but Lenny, the realist, insisted that tragic endings are more theatrical and memorable for the audience. Herbert reluctantly agreed, and they slaughtered her. If ever there was such a woman . . .*

Why am I speculating here? The world is full of them.

35

Claudia slept an exhausting, fitful sleep. Her internal clock was entirely misaligned, and it was already past lunchtime when she finally awoke. The bright daylight didn't bother her, but her hunger was a force to be reckoned with. The occasional meals Ms. Bertha had left at her door during her fierce work period barely sustained her, and now she felt the effects of malnutrition. A painful, gaping hole inside her stomach demanded to be filled. She craved a gigantic, old-fashioned breakfast, and as soon as she had dressed and tied her hair in a messy bun, she headed downstairs in search of food and coffee. At the bottom of the steps, a narrow white envelope on the hallway's round table caught her eye. It was elegantly propped against the decorative silver box, like a delicate museum exhibit. Strangely, it was addressed to her. She picked it up eagerly. It was a correspondence from the university, on official letterhead; it must have been urgent if it had reached her all the way here. She anxiously tore open the envelope and scanned the watermarked white cotton page.

Dear Ms. Morton,

The Department of Arts and Sciences of Grayland State University is pleased to announce the hiring of a full-time Associate Professor with a tenure-track, Dr. Mariko Utaka, who will be joining our faculty this Fall. Dr. Utaka is a graduate of the National Art Academy, the New England School of Modern Arts, and the New Century University, bringing an impressive experience in academic research with her visionary dissertation entitled "The Liberation of Compositional Processes and the Politics of Noise in Counterculture's Assertion of Influence over the Future Sonic Paradigm," as well as an exemplary record as an educator. Please join me in welcoming Dr. Utaka into our midst and show her the collegiality our institution is known for.

Because of this and other personnel changes, the Department is unable to extend your student employment contract into the fall semester. Dr. Utaka will be taking over the roster of your composition students, the Advanced Orchestration course, as well as the Music and Visual Arts Aesthetics in Post-Romantic Europe honors course. Please make arrangements to share any and all necessary materials related to the above-mentioned courses with Dr. Utaka as soon as possible.

As a courtesy, to aid you financially in completing your doctoral studies at our institution, the Department elects to offer you a position of lecturer until your thesis is completed, but not beyond the end of the Spring semester. In particular, we are pleased to offer you the Music Appreciation for Non-Majors course and coaching of woodwind chamber groups. The compensation for your work would be commensurate with entry-level courses and your decreased hour-load. Please inform me of your decision by the end of this month.

We wish you all the best with the final stretches of your doctoral dissertation and your imminent graduation. If you have any questions about the matter, please do not hesitate to contact me.

Cordially yours,
Robert Hurst
Dean of the College of Arts and Sciences

Claudia was speechless. She stood there, frozen, with her mouth fully open. No words came up to the surface. She uttered something between a scoff and a punctuated exhaling to finally break out in laughter. She could not believe his nerve. Was this a joke? How could Robert do this to her? Did Greg know about it? Claudia had always been their favorite adjunct professor. They had bent over backwards to keep her teaching. But the coveted tenure-track? Of course, they would never consider her. They wouldn't wait for her that long. She would have to graduate first, and after that, gather an additional five-to-seven years of teaching experience before her resume might float near to the top of the pile. And even then, they were not known for hiring their own students. They liked to dip into the vast pool of Ivy League graduates. They sought the prestige while trying to shake off the stigma of being a regional school.

Dear God, why had she not seen it coming? She had been naïve to assume they would extend her full teaching load until graduation. And those were her favorite courses—the Aesthetics course being of her own initiative and conception. And her composition students? They were perhaps the only reason she had hung on this long!

Everything was falling apart. Naturally, Claudia didn't want to pick up those leftover courses. No one wanted them. It might make more sense to take a job off-campus and simply finish her degree. The sooner, the better. Was this a sign? Sometimes a straightforward shutting of the door in one's face can be a sobering alternative to endless self-delusion. It looked like this letter had made a decision for her. Yet, on the fundamental level, what about the money, the health insurance? She had no savings. She was relying on this job to bring her through to graduation. This was not an easy pill to swallow, and the timing was atrocious.

Did Richard have something to do with this? Because she had refused to work for Adrienne? A cold shiver ran up her spine. Was he punishing her? He knew Greg. No doubt he knew the dean as well. The more she thought about it, the more horrified she became. It wouldn't surprise her if this was his doing. But this Utaka, she could not have just appeared out of nowhere, could she? Yes, the university had had a faculty search in place, but she never thought they would actually hire anyone until next year. Where was Utaka coming from? Claudia reread the dean's letter. The National Art Academy, the New England School of Modern Arts, and New Century University. Bingo! Adrienne's alma maters. Of course, it was all clear! They were pushing her out. She was a pawn in their grand scheme.

Claudia prepared a breakfast of scrambled eggs, bacon, and toast, and ate every bit of it slowly and deliberately until she was full and satisfied. She brought her orange juice out to the veranda to get some fresh air.

So, this was it, she thought; this was all she had left now. A couple of weeks left at Watershed, this forest, several crazed people who might not even be real, an unexpected new symphony in the midst of being born, and, as a bonus, possibly a mental illness. Everything else was falling away. Maybe it was meant to be; she never had the emotional stamina to compete in the Academic Olympics.

She should have been upset and panicking, but, strangely, she felt lighter, liberated. She smiled and took another sip of juice. She then returned to her room, slammed the door shut behind her, sat down at her desk, and continued writing. The music was more powerful and more unpredictable than ever.

36

Claudia uttered a long groan as she stretched her arms up in the air. She had just finished the symphony's third movement, with one more left to go. The music was still in draft form, a shorthand of sorts, but its foundations were solid. Knowing her intentions, Claudia could quickly copy it into the music notation software on her laptop to transform it into an intricate structure. That final stage would be less demanding, more like polishing the rough edges and bringing shine to a dull surface. She was satisfied with her work. And with the three movements behind her, she was confident she could still compose the final one, keeping nearly the same pace of the last few weeks.

She was a complete mess. She hadn't showered in two days, and her room was scattered with dirty clothes. Sheets were crumpled on the bed, and papers littered the floor, as did a few plates of dried and shriveled sausage and moldy tomatoes. She could smell the odor of her unwashed, greasy hair. It was time to take a break—to clean up a little, maybe even go for a walk outside, before her legs forgot entirely how to move. Without any social interactions, her anxiety was minimal, and she had stayed warm and protected in the cocoon of her room, yet now she was becoming restless, even lonely. She was ready to reemerge, to chat with someone again, and would happily let her thoughts entertain a topic other than music, however trivial. She could drop in on Diego and Victor to see how their projects had progressed.

But first, it was time to organize the manuscript. In the beginning, she had numbered the pages, but then, with time, neglected to continue doing so. Now she had to shuffle through her sketches to determine their correct order. She had scribbled several versions of the same passages on different sheets but had no trouble identifying which one was which. When she was finished, she stacked them neatly on the desk, and then started on organizing her clothes, with far less enthusiasm. She could tidy up in under three minutes, and yet these mundane chores debilitated her. How amusing that composing a symphony was within reach, but a quick cleanup of a bedroom seemed impossible.

As she picked up her sweatshirt and pajama pants, she looked through the window, across the courtyard. At the edge of the forest stood Symphony—with Gabriel. Claudia's heart skipped a beat. She wanted to run downstairs right then, and she would have done so were it not for the fact that she was dressed in an old T-shirt and underwear. A quick sprucing would do no good now. She needed a proper scrubbing, combing, toothbrushing, and flossing. But everything inside her ached to rush outside to greet him, to ask where he had been hiding all this time, to tell him about her work, the music, the bizarre events, everything.

She stood at the window, partially hidden behind the wall lest they look up and see her. She took a moment to observe the pair. Gabriel wore his regular work clothes and carried a brown messenger bag. He must have just arrived. He kept his hands in the pockets of his jacket and smiled affectionately at Symphony as she spoke, animatedly, to him. Claudia couldn't hear their conversation, but from their appearance could infer a close friendship. Symphony giggled, brushing her dark locks from her face. She kept motioning with her right hand while periodically touching Gabriel's arm with her left. At a certain point, she held on to him without letting go, still talking and gesticulating freely. He looked at her with great interest, laughing with her, never taking his eyes off her.

Was that it? Had Claudia missed this crucial element before? Was this what she had "misunderstood," or was this some brand new development? She had no reason to be jealous—he had never acted in an encouraging or a deceitful way toward her, never promised or implied anything—yet the sight of the two cooing struck a dissonant chord with her. She might talk to him later if he was still around. Or better yet, she could stay inside the villa to see if he came looking for her. She would simply have to let it take its course, just as Ms. Bertha had suggested.

But for now, she absolutely needed to wash and put on clean clothes. She would eat something and start a load of laundry. The mundane reality brought her back down to earth. She needed to stay productive, and physical activity would help to relieve her strained and tense mind.

She took a quick shower and washed and towel-dried her hair. Then, she put on a dress—the only clean article of clothing remaining—and went downstairs to the kitchen. She ate a late lunch: a turkey sandwich with lettuce and sprouts, and a small handful of potato chips with a cup of black tea. Later in the afternoon, she made several trips up- and downstairs, to wash two loads in the laundry room, to transfer them to the dryer, to iron a couple of shirts, to get another cup of tea, to check the hall table for new correspondence, to casually flip through music scores in the library, to get a glass of water from the kitchen, to walk up and down the main corridor for no reason at all. Gabriel never came. There was no trace of him.

37

"Claudia, excuse me, might we have a word? I see you've just finished your breakfast." Richard startled Claudia with an unexpected appearance in the kitchen doorway.

She grimaced and swallowed the last sip of coffee. She felt cornered and couldn't think of an excuse to postpone the meeting. She would have to suffer the fool one more time. She followed him to his office and took the chair he pointed her to. She promised herself she wouldn't play nice anymore and fidgeted impatiently.

"How has your stay been? I've been informed the last few weeks have been very productive for you. Is that right?" He assaulted her with his usual sunshine of a smile, but his folded hands on top of the desk signaled he was on official Foundation business.

"Yes, you could say I found my groove. I have been working at full steam," Claudia answered unenthusiastically, staring at him coldly.

"That's what we like to hear. This is what Watershed is known for, and that's why we always choose the best and the brightest."

He paused. That plastered-on smile. How did he do it?

"I have been in contact with Greg," he said casually. "He tells me they are hiring a new tenure-track professor." He looked at Claudia with concern. "And I hear this is going to affect you significantly. Have you now, in light of this new situation, given any more consideration to my offer?"

She scoffed and shrugged her shoulders. "I thought you withdrew your offer."

"Well, we could say it was temporarily withdrawn,"—he leaned back into the chair to pace his offensive—"but given your new circumstances, we might renew our negotiations, no?"

"What about Adrienne? Is she aware of this conversation? I thought she wasn't too keen on the idea." Claudia stood her ground, probing for more information.

"Claudia, I am offering you a straightforward transaction." He leaned toward her again, steepling his perfectly manicured fingers in a triangle of business sportsmanship. "I am able to convey to you twenty-five thousand dollars in exchange for your symphony and your confidentiality. I understand this amount might carry you through graduation and beyond."

Claudia looked at him without flinching. The bastard was serious. Although she had speculated in her mind as to the amount he might offer, she had never suspected it would be this much. It was a large chunk of change for her. She could pay her rent for months to come. She might not even have to work at all until graduation and could concentrate exclusively on her studies and her doctorate. The proposition was tempting, but she played it cool and held his gaze without looking away.

But, as any composer, she felt emotionally attached to her work. Could she give it away, just like that? Could she give her creativity child up for adoption? Abandon all contact? It seemed inhumane and cruel. But Victor had had no problem doing just that for the right price. Was she a fool to feel differently? Her mind spun in circles.

"Richard, I don't know what to say." She exhaled a breath she had been holding for too long. "This symphony is very personal to me. I'm not sure I can let it go."

"Everything has a price, Ms. Morton, but I hope you are not bargaining with me, are you? I have already invested a considerable sum into convincing you to write this thing to begin with."

"What do you mean?" she gasped, touching her throat.

"What I mean is that you are a very obstinate person, Claudia, very obstinate. That you require dramatic gestures and dire circumstances to elicit your creativity. This is very expensive to produce." The smile was gone. He looked annoyed.

"Dramatic gestures?" She didn't follow at all.

"Yes, it took a lot of synchronized effort and multiple confrontations to convince you to abandon your pathetic cello sonata in favor of writing a proper symphony. Do you think this would have happened on its own, without the help of your friends?" He motioned angrily toward the corridor. "Yes, I am aware of everything that goes on on this island, and I know what it took to cause you to finally make up your mind." He pointed at her with his index finger, as if he wanted to stab her.

She curled up her fists, sat on the edge of her chair, and leaned forward, ready with her counterattack. "I don't understand what you mean!" She pointed to her chest, owning every syllable: "It was my own choice to write the symphony. There may have been a few incidents that encouraged me to pursue this larger form, but the decision was my own. I only give credit to this island and the inspiration of the picturesque surroundings." With her large green eyes, she stared him down.

"Oh, please, don't be so deluded," he scoffed. "Do you think you pulled this inspiration out of thin air? Can't you tell your friends here—your fellow artists—have been working in concert to lead you to this point?" He walked from behind the desk and bent down in front of her face.

"I'm afraid I can't credit my fellow artists for working in concert." She leaned back and crossed her legs to create more space between them. "Their behavior has been rather erratic. I'm sure they have their own demons to fight and their own creative struggles to conquer without much concern for my own. And, to be honest, there have been times when I doubted their sanity." She finally had the guts to argue with him freely. It was empowering. She smiled triumphantly. "The young girl especially—Symphony, as she likes to call herself."

"Oh, Claudia, it all makes for an enchanting story, don't you think?" He sat on the desktop and crossed his arms. "A Symphony that begs to be written, a writer struggling with his novel, a painter who has lost color perception, all waiting with bated breath for you to complete your work or else they won't survive. The question is, did they cause you to doubt *your* sanity?"

Claudia didn't answer. Of course they had.

"Let me take the scales off your eyes, darling. Diego, Victor, and Stephanie are actors I hired for this little island experiment." He uncrossed his arms, bending down toward her again, towering over her. "Their sole purpose was to convince you to write the symphony and to write it very quickly in order to deliver it to me. Now, it is true, I cannot force you to give up the music, but I hope my offer is strong enough that you will find it tempting." He walked back behind the desk.

"Actors?" She pulled on her fingers. Her face soured.

"Yes, well, a painter, a writer, and a singer who

were willing to put on this little production in exchange for favorable reviews of their project grant applications. Art funding is difficult to come by these days, as you very well know. People can be quite creative when it comes to finding the right avenues." He was proud of his elaborate scheme.

"I don't know who's crazier, you or them!" Claudia had enough. She jumped up and started for the door.

"No, Claudia, what is crazy is the amount of effort it takes to make you write worthwhile music!" he yelled.

She stopped and spun around. "Richard, you and your hired friends are deranged fuck-ups! This island is fucked up!" she shouted, hand on her hip and gesticulating wildly. "And I bet you had everything to do with the hiring of Mariko Utaka and that you forced the dean's hand. I'm tired of you and this whole rigged system. You people are heartless, psychotic vultures!" She was livid.

"Be that as it may, my offer still stands." He was calm and collected. His unnerving smirk returned to his smug, revolting face. "I hope you will give it serious consideration so we can finally come to a mutually beneficial understanding."

The echo of his voice followed Claudia into the corridor as she stormed out of the office. Where could she go? She didn't want to return to her room. She needed a break from these confines. She had to find Gabriel. She would prefer not to be melodramatic, but she had to talk to him. Right now.

Richard hadn't mentioned him. Was he part of the deal—if there even was a deal? But if there wasn't, how had Richard known about the events at the river? Clearly, he had an informant. How did Gabriel fit into the picture? He was an outsider, so she doubted he had conspired in any way with the others. She had never even seen him with any of the others. Never? What about his conversation with Symphony—Stephanie?

Nothing made sense to Claudia anymore. Once again, her fluid world, like mercury escaping a glass thermometer, assumed any shape into which it was poured. She was wary of adjusting to ever-shifting layers of reality. It was hard enough to return to mundane tasks after a creative high, without being thrown into yet another act in this mind-warping circus. So, they were real? She was not crazy? They just made her believe she was? Was this not worse than the first option? Had she allowed them to manipulate her this whole time? She suspected Gabriel might hold the answers—that he might somehow help her, direct her, or at least listen without hostility or deceit. She needed him!

Running to the dock would be pointless. If he was on the island, he would be somewhere around the villa. She marched quickly toward the shed, the doors of which were wide open, revealing a workbench scattered with tools. She stepped inside and circled the parked blue truck, calling his name. No one answered. She walked back outside, clutching her sweater to her chest when the wind picked up and played with her long hair. She walked around the villa's perimeter, looking at the edges of the forest, into the clearings, inside the house through the windows. She finally stepped inside and went to the library. The room was empty and quiet. Diego and Victor sat together in the painter's studio, oblivious to her walking by. It was for the better. She was in no frame of mind to interact with them. She even peered into the office again, but Richard was already gone, and the only sound accompanying her now was the creaking of the floor under her feet.

Ms. Bertha peered out from the kitchen. "Are you looking for something, dear?" she asked, concerned.

"I don't know. I'm just trying to understand." Claudia didn't look at her and only waved her hand. She was lost, confused.

"You've been working very hard for a long time. Would you like to take a break? I made some soup. Are you ready for lunch?" She stepped out into the corridor.

"I had a late breakfast. Maybe later. Thank you."

Claudia darted away like a startled gazelle. She wanted to get back to her room before her tears had a chance to sting her face. She didn't want to be seen in a hysterical state. Not by Ms. Bertha, not by anyone. Damn this hypersensitivity!

38

Claudia could not remain in her room any longer. She had to get out. She was feeling claustrophobic, and her anxiety began to simmer again. The conversation with Richard and pondering her current financial prospects had much to do with it. Should she be smart about all this, like Ms. Bertha had suggested, and let go of her symphony and cash out? Could she compose another one later on, maybe even a better one? Now that she had proven she was capable of it, it seemed a viable option. And yet, she wasn't able to circumvent the thought that this whole proposed arrangement felt unethical.

She thought about Herbert, Rita, and their opera, wondering what had become of her. She didn't know Rita's last name but certainly couldn't recall any female composers from the 1960s or 1970s named Rita. She had relinquished her music for love or devotion to a man. Was it love? Money, no doubt, was also a factor. Did it help jumpstart her music career after the opera premiered? Claudia would have to do some research when she returned home.

But now? What to do now, with this precarious situation? She needed to earn money one way or another. It could be slow and painful, or quick and dirty. She didn't like the sound of either approach. She wished someone would make a decision for her, relieve her from the responsibility of being a grown-up, if only for a moment. Adult life was overrated.

She wandered downstairs without any aim or purpose. For now, she wanted to walk around, to let her thoughts find a proper rhythm. A stroll outside might be just what she needed, but the sound of a quiet conversation lured her to the library. Diego, Victor, and Stephanie sat in a half circle in front of the fireplace, and Diego was the first to hear her quiet approach.

"There you are! Join us, *Danaë*." Diego motioned for her to come in.

She entered slowly, unsure what to say or how to act. They turned to her, smiling, as if everything was in perfect order. He pulled another chair over for her, and they all scooted to make room for her in the center. She sat down reluctantly.

"So," she said, after a short pause, "we should probably talk." She stared at the cold, dormant fireplace.

"We can if you want to," said Victor. "What would you like to talk about?"

"Everything that happened, I suppose. Why it happened." Claudia was improvising her response as she went. "The truth about you, what is the meaning of . . ."

Her face froze as she caught sight of a large painting above the mantle. She stood up abruptly and stepped back to gain a proper perspective. The light from the side window cast a glare on its varnished surface, preventing her from ascertaining its subject, but a partial view of the figure gave her enough cause for concern. She stepped to the left and to the right until she found a clear viewpoint. And then, a jolt of horror flushed through her veins as she recognized herself in the artwork.

The painting depicted her entirely nude and unencumbered, lying on a bed in full-frontal display. The sheets wove playfully between her thighs in a suggestive way, covering one of her knees but completely exposing her pubic hair. Her legs were spread as if in a weightless, epic jump or pirouette, and her left arm reached out widely, enticing the viewer to enter her company. Her hair floated in all directions, making her into a grotesque mythical creature, a romanticized erotic nymph. If not for the Pre-Raphaelite style in which the painting had been fashioned, it could have been mistaken for a modern shampoo ad. Claudia's face, with an alluring, nonchalant smile and half-closed eyes, glowed in ecstasy, while her moist, shiny lips and tongue caressed a dark red cluster of cherries she held with her right hand. Burgundy juice flowed from the pierced fruit onto her wrist and neck, all the way to her chest, between her pale adolescent breasts, perked up without inhibition. Claudia was shocked, devastated. She felt utterly violated.

"How could you, Diego?" she whispered. She didn't have the strength for an outburst. "I can't believe it. How could you do this after you knew how I . . . ?" She slumped over, touching her knees.

"That's a beautiful painting," Victor chimed in. They all remained seated in their half circle, looking at the artwork. "The light isn't very good right now, but look at the colors. The flesh tones are so vivid, and the juice!" He laughed out loud.

"Well, I think it's pretty. You look like a goddess," said Stephanie with adoration. "I really like it."

"I didn't consent to this. You had no right to paint it!" Claudia's voice quivered.

Diego stood up and turned around. "Please don't be upset. I thought that once you saw it, you would understand how beautiful you are. I mean, this is a terrific piece of art, if I may say so myself." His features contorted. He wasn't hiding his disappointment in her reaction very well.

"Do you think I don't know what's going on here? All your schemes, your manipulations, your conspiracy!" She bore down on them, distraught and shaking, and they turned to face her. "Richard told me all about it."

"Oh, don't take it so personally," Victor dismissed her, keeping his hands in his pockets. "We're all in this together. It's a creative process, bouncing ideas off one another. Isn't that what this retreat is all about?" He was annoyed with her again.

"Not for me." Claudia shook her head and began to pace. "You've been playing your charades this whole time at my expense." She wouldn't be docile and congenial anymore. "Is this what Richard is paying you for? All this drama, the pretense? Is he paying you for this painting? Is he paying you to bully me and mistreat me, to humiliate me?" She was getting better at raising her voice, advocating on her own behalf.

"Oh, come on, don't play the victim here. No one has hurt you!" Diego was agitated. "If anything, we gave you space to work undisturbed. You're definitely too temperamental and overemotional. You have a tendency to blow everything out of proportion. You imagine things!"

He pulled the painting angrily off the mantle and set it on the floor, leaning it against the bookcase. In the new setting, the portrait was even more vivid, vibrant, lifelike.

"Am I imagining this painting you made categorically against my will? Did I imagine your breakdown, Symphony—Stephanie, whatever your name is? Have I imagined your psychological manipulations, Victor?" Claudia shouted.

Victor scoffed, but Stephanie kept quiet, holding on to the back of her chair and looking at Claudia with her large brown eyes, visibly hurt.

"I've had enough of you people!" Claudia

yelled. "I'm tired of this theater, this circus!" She waved her arms erratically. "Don't think I'll be your main attraction, or a subject in your experiment, anymore!"

She stormed out of the room. It was time to leave the island once and for all. And yes, the ferry was due to arrive in the afternoon, and the weather this time was perfect.

Just as she was heading to the stairs to pack, the front door opened to Richard and a tall blond woman. She was formidable and elegant and carrying a designer handbag in the crook of her elbow. She might have been lifted out of a *Vogue* spread.

"Ah, Claudia!" Richard grinned cheerfully. "Good! Meet my daughter, Adrienne." The woman reached out to her with a wide, warm smile, offering her hand. Claudia was startled, uncertain what to do, and she began to turn around, but Victor came up right behind her, trapping her. She was surrounded from all sides.

"Victor! Pumpkin!" Adrienne's attention shifted immediately. She squealed in euphoric delight, rushing past Claudia to greet him, and Victor opened his arms to catch her, lifting her off her feet and twirling her. She locked her thighs around his hips and kissed his face repeatedly while mussing his dark wavy hair.

39

"Claudia, it's so good to finally meet you! Dad has told me so much about you." Adrienne's presence was palpable, the scent of her musky perfume almost tangible. Energetic and upbeat, she had the aura of a television personality. Claudia felt dwarfed in comparison.

"It's nice to meet you, too," she replied quietly.

"We have a lot to talk about. I want to hear all about you, your stay here, your work—everything!" She smiled warmly, profusely. This was not how Claudia had imagined her at all.

"Look, I don't know what Richard has told you, but we've had some tumultuous disagreements and some curious developments here at Watershed."

Claudia felt her arm being gently guided by Adrienne as they entered the office. Before she realized what was happening, she was seated at the desk opposite Richard, with Adrienne beside her.

"That doesn't surprise me at all. The creation of art is tumultuous. The music business is tumultuous. I'm hoping we can find common ground and come up with a solution that benefits everyone." She sounded just like her father. She was a born saleswoman, a dealer, a closer.

"Dad told me you've made great progress on the symphony and that you're ready to develop the final version?" Adrienne relaxed in her chair, with her legs crossed and resting her elbows on the armrests, confidently open to all opportunities that might present themselves. She wore a short gray leather skirt that exposed her smooth, spray-tanned knees, and a white blouse adorned with a chunky silver necklace. She looked dry-cleaned and expensive.

"I have yet to compose the fourth movement, but I think I'm nearly finished with the first three. I have to write out the full orchestration, that's all." Claudia, wearing a gray hoodie and a pair of old jeans, was out of her league, but at least she had her intellect and her accomplishments.

"Well, then. It's a good moment to celebrate and seal the deal! What do you think, Claudia?" Adrienne chirped enthusiastically. "Can you have the entire symphony all finished in another four weeks? You can complete it at home, but we should finalize the agreement today."

"What agreement is that?" Claudia asked carefully.

Richard, for the first time, was quiet. He was taking immense pride in observing his daughter in action.

"I have a standard nondisclosure agreement here." Adrienne pulled a packet out of her briefcase. She opened the yellow envelope and laid the document on the desk in front of Claudia. Pink sticky notes dangled from the edges, marking spaces reserved for her signature. "It basically outlines that you were hired to produce this work and that you are obligated, under financial penalty, to remain quiet about the agreement." Adrienne recited this part mechanically. She didn't seem to be in virgin territory.

"That's just about it." She shrugged. "Lots of fine print, but those are the main points."

"I don't know . . . I don't think . . . I mean, I haven't made my decision yet." Claudia looked at the stack of papers.

"I understand, but there isn't much time left before the competition deadline,"—Adrienne leaned in, speaking softly—"and we should have this documentation in place as soon as possible."

"I'm not sure this is the right thing for me to do. It might be best if you found someone else. There must be other composers better suited . . ." Claudia tried to backpedal.

"I see you are hesitant, and I do understand." Adrienne sat up straight, holding an imaginary box in her hands. "Father and I are prepared to offer you thirty thousand dollars, but only if you sign the agreement today. Time is of the essence, you see." She looked at Claudia sternly, without blinking.

Claudia was besieged. Adrienne handed her a pen, and she took it dutifully. She lifted the pages and scanned them with her eyes.

"I have to at least read it first. It's a long document," she mumbled.

"Of course, take your time. And if you have any questions, we can discuss all your concerns." Adrienne was reassuring, nurturing.

Claudia felt her body softening. The antique clock on the shelf ticked softly, dividing time into thin, manageable slices. She didn't think about the symphony so much as she thought about the thirty thousand dollars and what she could do with it. She could begin paying off her student loans, she could move to Manhattan, take an exotic vacation. She could even buy a car.

"It's certainly very tempting," Claudia admitted with a faint smile. "I have heard about work-for-hire agreements before."

"Don't do it, Claudia." Gabriel stood in the doorway to the office.

"What are you doing here? This doesn't concern you," said Adrienne.

"Everything that concerns her music concerns me," Gabriel replied coldly. He lowered his messenger bag to the floor and approached the desk.

Claudia snapped out of her trance. She could stand up and throw herself into his embrace. Where had he been all this time? She wanted to tell him about her major breakthrough, about the turmoil, but instead she only sat there motionless, half-paralyzed.

"Symphony told me about the letter from your

university." Gabriel looked at Claudia with concern. "Don't believe it. They fabricated it."

Symphony, right behind him, was holding on to Gabriel's elbow as if to steady herself. She glanced pleadingly at Claudia, before shaking her head.

"I resent your accusations!" Richard jumped up and placed his palms firmly on the desk's surface.

"Please, don't do it, Claudia. Don't sell me," Symphony whispered. She was on the verge of tears.

Claudia slowly stood up, documents and pen in hand.

"How did the letter get here? Ask them how it arrived." Gabriel pointed at them.

She looked at Adrienne, then at Richard, then back to Gabriel.

"What do you care how it arrived? It came with the mail," said Richard, annoyed.

"I bring the mail from the mainland post office once a week," said Gabriel resolutely. "If there was a letter addressed to you, I would have known about it." He took a step toward Claudia.

"But you were gone, Gabriel. You were gone for three weeks," she pleaded.

"I wasn't gone. I was here every Friday with the mail, like always. It was you who was gone, swept away by the music. You didn't see me, but I was here twice, sometimes three times a week, checking on you each time. You were working so intently, I didn't want to disturb you. But I can tell you there was no letter addressed to you." His voice trembled. He stood in front of her, grasping his thighs as if to restrain himself.

"But the watermarked pages and the university logo?" Claudia argued.

"How hard do you think it is for them to get some stationary from a university to which they have easy access?" He faced Richard and Adrienne.

Claudia placed the papers and the pen on the desk. "I won't be signing anything today," she said calmly.

"Let's go. The ferry will be here in forty-five minutes. You shouldn't stay here anymore." Gabriel put his arm around Claudia and escorted her to the door.

"Well, this is certainly much more drama than any of us anticipated. An interesting culmination." Victor was now standing behind Symphony in the overcrowded office.

"Please, spare me your writerly narratives," Claudia muttered and pushed Victor aside. She made her way out, and Gabriel and Symphony followed.

"No harm done. We all got what we came here for," Victor replied, chuckling. "I have my novel, Diego has his painting, and you have your symphony. It just took a few extra twists of the plot to accomplish it." He shouted after her as she neared the staircase. "Don't be angry. It's just a bit of playful drama!"

"Are you with them or are you with us?" Adrienne hissed through her clenched teeth, following Victor out into the hallway.

"I'm not with anyone. I'm just an observer," he laughed again, lifting his hands in defense.

"I'll help you with your luggage once you finish packing," Gabriel called to Claudia as she walked upstairs.

"I won't be long," she said.

"Are you just going to let her go like this?" Adrienne yelled at Victor.

"What do you want me to do? Even I'm surprised by this ending, and I'm the novelist here." He wasn't laughing anymore. "You can antagonize your protagonist only so long before she turns on you."

40

Gabriel carried Claudia's suitcase onto the veranda.

"Wait here," he instructed her. "I'll get the truck from the shed."

Claudia understood that he would be dropping her off at the main ferry dock, but secretly she hoped he would take her out on his boat one last time to bring her to the mainland himself.

"Claudia, thank you for everything you have done for me." Symphony came up to her. "You don't even know how much it means to me."

"Don't mention it. Isn't that what composers are for? And I hope you can forgive me for . . ." she hesitated.

"There is nothing to forgive. We had a rocky start, but the end result was worth it."

Symphony reached out to her, opening her arms. Claudia reciprocated, and they embraced firmly. The sincerity of the girl moved Claudia to tears.

"Goodbye, Symphony," she said. "I wish you the best, always."

"No, not quite goodbye yet. You still have to

finish the final movement." Symphony held Claudia's hand.

"Yes, I suppose you're right." Claudia smiled, wiping away her tears.

"We have to be going, Claudia," Gabriel called up to her from the bottom of the veranda stairs.

In one swift motion, he grabbed her laptop bag and her manuscript portfolio and placed them on the truck bed. Her suitcase was already there. He guided her to the passenger seat, closed the door behind her, and they took off without delay. Claudia looked back through the cabin's rear window. Symphony was still there, waving. Claudia waved back, overtaken by a feeling of loss. She should have done more to reach out to the woman, to get to know her better. She regretted dismissing her, not taking her more seriously.

Gabriel took the same road along which Victor had driven Claudia on that first day. She looked around for the last time. The foliage was now slightly thinner but more colorful, showing signs that the season was already turning. The trees and shrubbery remained in the old, familiar spots, yet everything was new.

"I have so much to tell you, Gabriel." Claudia sighed. "So much has happened in the last three weeks, you wouldn't believe it if I told you."

Gabriel smiled but kept his eyes on the road. She wished they could spend more time together, to talk, to explore nature, to just be.

"I think I would believe you. Symphony has filled me in on everything. I heard you had quite a prolific time with her. She was very complimentary of your progress."

"This place, this villa, the forest, everything that happened. . . . I couldn't understand it at first, and I'm still not sure I really get it, but I can't argue with the music I've written." Claudia was bubbly and animated. "I've never composed like this before. I feel liberated and empowered!"

"I'm thrilled to hear it!" And he was genuinely happy for her, smiling warmly. He slapped the steering wheel. "From the sound of it, it looks like Watershed gave you everything you came for."

"Yes, it did. I got so much more than I expected but . . ." She paused, ". . . somehow it's still not enough . . ." She looked at him, unsure of the right words.

"It's never enough, Claudia. That's the fundamental predicament of every artist. That's what keeps you awake at night, what propels you forward to new ideas." He stared straight ahead.

"And what about you, Gabriel? What propels you?" she asked, and now, for a split second, he turned toward her.

"What propels me is helping you realize that you have it in you to create, and to bring into existence everything your mind imagines. My belief in you propels me. I would do anything within my power to help you understand it."

"You always speak in such general, metaphysical terms." She looked away, resting her elbow on the window, disheartened he didn't see her the way she wanted him to.

"They are not general. They are very practical for me. I am here to guide you and to watch over you. I think I've done quite well so far, wouldn't you say?"

"You have done well. I am grateful," Claudia answered quietly, with a bittersweet smile.

The truck made a sharp turn, and they reached the end of the gravel road connecting to the dock. They unloaded in silence, and he carried her luggage onto the pier. He leaned her manuscript folio against the suitcase and handed her the laptop bag.

"Do you think we might be suited to become a team? That is, if the results are to your liking?" he asked tentatively. His eyebrows furrowed and his lips parted.

Claudia didn't expect such an offer. A team? What did he mean by that? The river stood still, but the sun danced impatiently across its surface. Claudia's heart beat faster as she began to understand. The realization was ripe, vibrant, and immensely frightening.

"This island has warped my mind a few times already, and I'm still not clear which side of reality we are in right now. I'm trying to grasp the dynamics of this place. Do you work for Richard? Are you with them, or against them?" She stuck her balled fists in her pockets to steady herself, to keep her conflicting emotions in check.

"Don't think in those terms. We are all rooting for you and we all want you to succeed. We just have different ways of going about it." He stood beside her, facing the open water. He measured his words carefully. "You have a rare talent in need of strengthening and encouragement. That kind of quality isn't born out of academic or institutional learning. It is revealed in adversity, in introspection, in personal struggle, in despair, solitude. An artist needs a safe place to work out her inner demons, to set a stage, to test various scenarios. And that's what we gave you. We are the pieces on your game board."

"Pieces on a game board? Are you speaking allegorically again?" She looked toward the bottom of the riverbed.

Gabriel stepped right in front of her, so she had no choice but to look at him.

"Oh, Claudia, poetry isn't your strong suit, is it?" He sighed, but his bright eyes and guarded smile betrayed his affection for her.

"I'm afraid not. I think I do better with facts and logic." She wasn't amused.

"Well, in that case, let me say plainly: I would like you to consider me for the role of your Muse. You have reached that stage, Claudia. It's time." He stood stock straight, his arms at his sides, like a soldier.

"My what?" She snorted but regretted it instantly when she saw she had hurt his feelings. "I'm sorry, but I still don't follow."

"It looks like you may need more time to process everything that has happened. It's understandable," Gabriel said, calmly, and he looked back to the river.

The sound of the ferry approaching reminded Claudia of her impending departure, and a wave of grief swept through her in a cold gush.

He squeezed her narrow shoulders, allowing her to feel the weight of his large hands. She held on to his wrist and sank into his sheltering embrace. She buried her face in his chest.

"All I'm saying is that I'm here for you and that I believe in you," he whispered tenderly. He kissed the top of her head, and then gently let her go.

"Thank you, Gabriel. I wish we had a little more time." Her eyes teared and her throat tightened.

"Goodbye for now, Claudia. Please think about what I said."

"Gabriel . . ." Words eluded her. "I'll miss you."

She boarded the ferry and faced the island as the boat pulled her away. He stood on the pier, watching her, immovable, until he became a distant tiny speck. But his calm face was imprinted on Claudia's mind, and her heart was filled with wonder and an unnamed sorrow.

41

Claudia scanned the bus schedule. She still had an hour and a half before she could continue on to the train station in Albany. A small diner across the street looked like a good place to kill some time, especially since she was ravenous. From the outside, it looked like a typical greasy spoon, with blue-and-red neon lights blinking at travelers and locals alike. The dining room seemed empty, and this simple fact was enough to convince her not to look any farther. The waitress was about to seat her when Claudia noticed a familiar face at a table in the back corner. A bearded man wearing a green plaid shirt sat alone, chewing on a hamburger, and with a paper napkin wiping the grease and ketchup dripping from the corners of his mouth.

"Brian? Is that you?" she asked, approaching his table. "I'm sorry, do you mind?" She motioned to the waitress, who let her wander off.

"Claudia! What on earth are you doing in my corner of the world?" He was caught off guard, scratching his cheek and sipping on his soda through a straw.

"Your corner? I could ask you the same thing."

Claudia was delighted to see a familiar face.

"My mom lives on Overlook Island. I'm on my way to visit her for the weekend. I thought I would stop in here for some real food. Mom doesn't approve, you know." He pointed at the burger and laughed. He pushed his dishes to the side to make room for Claudia.

"How's the photography business?" she asked, getting situated and taking off her jacket.

"Oh, you know, as well as it can be for us purists who refuse to go digital and still insist on poisoning our bodies with chemicals. I'm working on a new show for the winter. I thought I would take some shots of the river through the turn of the seasons."

"It's the perfect time for it," Claudia agreed.

"Overlook Island has gotten too touristy for my taste, too gentrified. I need to find something more pristine. I'm going to use Mom's canoe and scout the area for some scenery."

Claudia nodded and smiled.

"But what about you? What are you doing here?" he asked, rocking back and forth.

"I'm returning from an artist retreat," she answered.

"Wait, don't tell me. Watershed? You were able to get into the program?" His eyes widened.

"Yes. Have you heard about it?"

"Are you kidding me? That place is legendary—very guarded by the owner. I applied a couple of times but only made it to the waiting list. That woman has quite a reputation." He toyed with his utensils on his cleaned plate.

"What do you mean 'a reputation'?" Claudia asked.

"Well, it's not exactly like that villa is on the radar of major art institutes scouting for glamorous residencies." He bent toward her and lowered his voice conspiratorially. "But the insiders have been buzzing about it for decades. It's *the* place for serious artists to find themselves, but not something you would necessarily put on a resume, if you know what I mean. But you know all that. How was it for you?" He eyed her expectantly.

"I had a very productive time, you could say." She rested her chin on her hand.

"Oh, come on, give me some scraps." He wiped his forehead impatiently. "I'm dying to find out more about that place."

"I'm not sure what to tell you." Claudia looked out the window onto the busy street full of passing cars and pedestrians. "I'm still trying to process everything. It was a unique collection of artists, and yes, I did have a breakthrough, and so did they." She glanced back at him and grinned.

"*They?* I've heard it's just a small villa with one guest bedroom in the attic. Did the woman do some expansions or remodeling to house more participants?"

"The downstairs is quite large. I don't know, I didn't think much about it." She ran her finger around the rim of her water glass.

"Well, maybe she did something different this year. But I've heard that for a long time, she would only take one artist at a time, maybe twice a year, and that's why it was always so impossible to get in. From what I was told, that was the whole point—for the artist to be totally isolated, to create undisturbed." He paused and nodded. "What did you work on?"

"I wrote a symphony," Claudia answered carefully, but she was brimming with happiness.

"Way to go! Wow, that's quite an undertaking!" he exclaimed.

"Tell me more about what you know of Watershed," Claudia probed. "I'm curious how it compares with my experience."

"But you haven't told me much yourself. How was the island? Is there really something magical about it, like people say? There have been so many stories—from a fugitive chased by the FBI, to Bigfoot, to old Rita going insane, and everything in between."

"Wait, what? Rita?" Claudia perked up. "What do you know about her?"

"Well, people in these parts have been gossiping about her for years. I don't know if there's any truth to it at all." He rested his elbows on the table, leaned in, and lowered his voice. "But apparently Rita broke up the marriage of some big composer in New York in the 1960s. She was in the music scene herself, but disappeared around the same time he did, so you can draw your own conclusions. The funny part is, no one can figure out why the composer's widow left everything to Rita in her will. I mean, what woman would do something like that for her husband's mistress?"

"Rita? Rita owns Watershed?" Claudia's eyes widened. "I thought it was Ms. Bertha."

"I think Rita is her name, but yeah, she goes by 'Ms. Bertha' now. My mom knows her as Rita. She hasn't seen her in years, though. The woman keeps mostly to herself. What was she like? Was she spooky and weird?" he asked.

"No, she was elegant and soft-spoken. I didn't see her very much at all." Claudia looked away, dazed. "Now I wish I made more of an effort. The whole arrangement was . . . she gave me so much space . . ."

"Yes, that's what I've heard!" He livened up. "She gives the space to an artist, cooks for them, leaves them alone, and *poof*, the magic happens!"

"What else do you know about her?" Claudia asked.

"I don't know, just shreds of hearsay. Apparently, she inherited everything from the composer's wife—the villa and his manuscripts. That for a long time she was the official trustee and administrator of his music, and that she brought to light previously undiscovered compositions and published them posthumously. Now, she only runs the Watershed Foundation and makes it her mission to help random artists."

Claudia said nothing. She was lost in her thoughts, shaking her head.

"Well, listen, I hate to rush off like this, but my ferry is about to take off," the man said. "Please stay in touch and definitely come to my show in the winter." He dropped two twenty-dollar bills on the table. "Here, dinner is on me."

"Yes, take care. Thank you. Good luck," Claudia replied, still bewildered, hardly noticing when he left.

She sat there motionless, pondering everything he just told her and comparing it to what she had experienced at Watershed. She weighed what was objectively real against that which was not. She thought about the definition of reality and what it meant to her. She reached for her manuscript portfolio and pulled out a few pages of her music. There, in her own handwriting, was the final sketch of the symphony she had worked on so relentlessly. She sifted through the pages. Everything was there in the order she had arranged it. All the scribbles, all the drafts, all the notes, numbered, logically assembled.

A white piece of paper slipped from between the pages. On it, drawn in pencil, was a portrait of an attractive young woman with dark wavy hair and a voluptuous figure, seated in an armchair. Claudia remembered that pose from her session with Diego when Symphony joined in. But Claudia was absent from the drawing. Instead, Symphony was seated comfortably in the middle of the chair, all by herself, smiling, content. Claudia pushed the pages back into the portfolio and zipped it tightly. She clutched it close to her body, reassured the music was still inside. Yes, it was all there, and much more still bubbling in her mind, waiting to spill out. She was ready to dive deeper.

About the Author

Dosia McKay is an American composer of music for concert stage, film, and modern dance. Her portfolio includes works for symphony orchestra, chamber ensembles, choir, soloists, as well as electro-acoustic installations. Her music has been featured on National Public Radio and in concerts throughout the United States, including New York and Washington, D.C., and in Poland, China, Spain, Argentina, and others. She has released full-length albums: *Lacrimosa*, *Glossolalia*, and *Endless Immersion*, as well as several singles. Dosia is also a painter concentrating on portraiture and abstract expressionist imagery. She has published a collection of poems, short stories, and essays on her blog *Music Well*. *The Flow* is her debut novel.

www.DosiaMcKay.com

If you have enjoyed *The Flow*, please consider leaving a review in the online store where you purchased the book and share your experience on social media. Thank you for supporting independent artists.

Made in the USA
Middletown, DE
07 June 2020